"Everyone, if I ṁ ṁ attention."

Judah's voice rang out across the ballroom, stopping music and movement and turning all eyes toward them. His arm at her waist was a band of steel, keeping her in place, but why? What was he doing?

"First, I'd like to welcome you all here tonight. I appreciate the time and trouble so many of you have taken to get here."

A waiter approached them with a tray full of drinks and he took one and passed it to her before collecting another for himself. "Second, I'd like to introduce one particular woman to you all. A woman whose name you will have no doubt heard in connection with mine even if you haven't met her personally. A woman of rare compassion and resilience. Someone who has seen the darkest actions mankind has to offer and yet somehow manages to retain her sanity and goodness."

He couldn't possibly be talking about her.

"Someone who inspired me to look outward rather than in, at a time when all I could see were concrete walls and prison bars. Ladies and gentlemen, please raise your glasses to Bridie Starr." He smiled down at her, all shark. "My future wife."

Say *what*?

Kelly Hunter has always had a weakness for fairy tales, fantasy worlds and losing herself in a good book. She has two children, avoids cooking and cleaning and, despite the best efforts of her family, is no sports fan. Kelly is, however, a keen gardener and has a fondness for roses. Kelly was born in Australia and has traveled extensively. Although she enjoys living and working in different parts of the world, she still calls Australia home.

Books by Kelly Hunter

Harlequin Presents

Claimed by a King

Shock Heir for the Crown Prince
Convenient Bride for the King
Untouched Queen by Royal Command
Pregnant in the King's Palace

Visit the Author Profile page
at Harlequin.com for more titles.

RETURN OF THE
OUTBACK BILLIONAIRE

Some rise by sin, and some by virtue fall.

—William Shakespeare, *Measure for Measure*

PROLOGUE

THE RED RIVER GUM floorboards in the ballroom gleamed with the shine of fresh beeswax polish and the soft glow cast by dozens of antique wall sconces. Every set of doors along the generous expanse of wall to the west stood open to the veranda beyond, even if doing so would provide scant protection from the night moths drawn towards the light. The rest of the homestead at the heart of Jeddah Creek station had been dusted, buffed and made to look like the expensive Victorian-era folly it was. Whoever had thought to bring white wrought-iron features and open verandas into the middle of a red desert landscape bloated with dust, drought and a fiercely relentless sun had been quite mad. That or English and dreaming of the world they'd left behind.

Judah Blake often wondered how long it had taken his English ancestors to realise people dreamed so very differently here.

He'd been back a little over a week, and if he still found going through an open door or eating whatever he felt like whenever he felt like it a challenge,

he liked to think he kept those challenges to himself.
He'd been born and raised on Jeddah Creek station;
he knew this harsh land and all its wonders. He'd
conquer being back here soon enough.

His eighteen-year-old brother, Reid, had been
the one to suggest some kind of party to celebrate
Judah's return. Judah had been the one to turn his
brother's modest suggestion into a society ball. He'd
needed to know just how much damage his impris-
onment had done to his family's standing, and what
better way than to send out invitations to a big char-
ity ball and see who showed up?

He'd spared no expense—no one would ever com-
plain of his hospitality. Whatever a guest wanted to
drink, they would find it here. The food had been
flown in alongside catering staff and musicians. A
small army of cleaners, tradesmen and a couple of
event co-ordinators had spent the week preparing
the homestead to receive guests. Stock hands had
spent days setting out a parking area for all the private planes and helicopters those guests would arrive in. Not all the guests would be wealthy. Some
would arrive in little outback helicopters more suited
to mustering cattle than providing luxury transport.
Some would bring the family Cessna, the outback
equivalent of a family car. Jeddah Creek station ran
straight across the border between Queensland and
the Northern Territory and was a nightmare to get
to by road.

And yet, out of the several hundred invitations

he'd sent out at short notice, only a handful had been declined.

He could blame some of that willingness to accommodate him on his family name. His father had been a member of the English aristocracy—a lowly baron who had married the daughter of a viscount and fled to Australia to escape the sanctimonious superiority of her relatives. But his parents were dead, one after the other, these past six months, and Judah was *the* Blake now, with all the fealty it entailed.

He could blame some of the attendance on the fact that he'd been blessed with a handsome face, wasn't yet thirty, and wasn't yet married. And he was rich—Old Money rich, even if his recently deceased father had burned through most of it. He also had thirty billion dollars' worth of New Money, courtesy of two cryptocurrency investments he'd made at just the right time. He'd tried to keep that windfall quiet, but in the rarefied world of one-percenters there were always some who made it their business to know which way the money flowed.

And that, above all, was why so many people had chosen to show their faces here tonight. With thirty billion dollars sitting in his back pocket, it apparently really *was* going to be that easy for the same people who'd ignored him for more than seven years to step up now, forgive him his sins and welcome him back into the fold.

Amazing how many of them had already been in contact on account of investment possibilities that might be of interest to him. Good causes, all. Could only help him restore his tarnished reputation, they'd implied, and he'd smiled fierce and flat and told them he looked forward to catching up with them soon.

They had no idea what kind of man he'd become. *He* had no idea what kind of man he would be now that he was out and blessed with more wealth than he knew what to do with and so many open doors.

All he knew was that he wanted everything back the way it was. His parents alive. His soul not yet stained by what it took to get along in a cage, but it was too late for that. Nor was he ever likely to will his parents back to life.

Retrieving the parts of Jeddah Creek station his father had sold off, though…that was something he *could* set right. His birthright and his solace. *His* land, not Bridie Starr's.

'Don't do anything rash once you get out,' the visiting psych expert had said in the days before his release.

As if Judah hadn't spent the past seven years and then some learning to control his every thought and feeling.

'Avoid split-second decisions.'

Guess the doc had never had an inmate with a shiv heading towards him, fast and furtive.

'Give yourself time to adjust.'

This sounded like halfway good advice.

'Your reading of people will be off. Give others the benefit of the doubt.'

Like hell he would.

Bridie Starr had taken temporary possession of land that belonged to him and the fix was very simple—nothing rash about it.

He wanted it back.

CHAPTER ONE

'DO YOU KNOW what you're going to wear?'

'I haven't decided yet.' Bridie Starr stared despondently at the lemon meringue pie Gert had whipped up seemingly out of nowhere and wondered, not for the first time, where the other woman had learned to cook. Not around here, that was for sure. Here being the channel country of central Australia, and far, far away from any kind of crowd. Bridie had been born and raised here on Devil's Kiss station. Gert hailed from Barcoo, a few hundred kilometres to the south. Neither place tended to grow master chefs.

Gert arrived at Bridie's homestead for three days every fortnight and made the place bright with beeswax, laughter, shared cooking and conversation, before heading next door to Jeddah Creek station to do the same for the Blakes. A two-day stint with the Conrads to the north, and then Gert would return to her home and set up to make the trip all over again.

Gert was the glue that kept people around here connected.

'I'm not sure I even want to go to the Blakes' ball,' Bridie confessed.

'Can't say I'm surprised.'

And why should she be? Bridie's shut-in tendencies weren't exactly a secret.

'But you have to go,' the older woman continued briskly. 'People will be looking to you to see what you'll do now that Judah's back. It'd be cruel to act as if you're scared of him.'

'I'm not scared of him.' And she didn't want to be cruel. 'It's just…why did he have to go and throw a society ball, of all things? Out here?'

Gert's thin lips stretched into a smile. 'Used to be a time when fancy balls were all the rage at Jeddah Creek station, you're just too young to remember them. They put on at least one a season and all the fancy types would be there. The things we got up to…' The older woman sounded positively wistful. 'Your mother loved them. She and your father used to dance all night long, and they were good at it.'

Bridie's mother had left the world not long after Bridie had set foot in it. Gert was the only person who ever talked freely about her.

Her father never spoke of his wife at all.

Okay, so her mother had loved dancing and balls. Maybe Bridie could learn to love them too. She'd already RSVP'd that she and her father would be there. No way could they stay away after everything Judah had done for her. And she had to be presentable, which wouldn't be hard, what with a closet full of rarely worn designer clothes at her fingertips, all of them tailored just for her. Granted, they were half a dozen years out of date, but haute couture never really dated. All the age of a piece did was show other people for how long someone had been obscenely wealthy.

Bridie didn't consider her wealth obscene, but once upon a time she'd modelled such clothes and sometimes she'd been allowed to keep them. She'd been a rising star with the face of an angel and a body on the cusp of womanhood. She'd had absolutely no clue about the predators roaming the glittering, crazy world of high-fashion modelling.

Her awakening had been a hard one.

'What did people used to wear to these balls? Full formal?'

'Absolutely.'

'Breast medals and sashes and things? Gloves for the women?'

'No to the medals and sashes, yes to the family rings and jewels, sometimes gloves,' answered Gert. 'Landed gentry and all that. Sometimes it's subtle, but it does show.'

Bridie blew out a frustrated breath as she tried to mentally turn Judah next door into Lord Judah Blake, peer of the realm, bona fide English aristocracy. 'Right, then. Gown time. She pushed a hand through the thick waves of summer-wheat-coloured hair, liberally sprinkled with darker shades of brown, and vowed yet again to get a proper haircut before the ball.

'He phoned this morning wanting to speak to you.'

'Judah?' She'd been dodging his calls all week.

'So ring him back.'

She nodded, knowing full well that returning his call would take more guts than she had. At least at the ball they'd be surrounded by people and the conversation wouldn't get too personal too fast. Ease into things slowly was her motto.

'You're not going to call him back, are you?' stated Gert flatly.

'No. But I will be at the ball, dressed to impress, and I *will* speak with him then and welcome him home and shower him with gratitude and whatever else I need to do. Trust me, Gert, I have a plan.'

'Good girl,' soothed the older woman. 'Have some pie.'

Something was up. Gert never let anyone at the lemon meringue pie before it was cool, but she cut Bridie a slice and watched with barely contained disapproval as the warm filling oozed all over the plate.

'Now.' The older woman's steely gaze could have skewered a razorback at a hundred paces. 'Let's get this sorted, sweet petal.'

Sweet petal… Oh, this was bad. Worse than when Bridie had used the giant Limoges vase that used to sit at the end of the hallway as a frisbee target… and nailed it.

'What are you going to wear?'

* * *

Judah watched from his vantage point at one end of the ground-floor veranda as his guests spilled out of the crowded ballroom and into the night to speak in glowing terms of the landscape they'd flown over to get here and the beauty of the old two-storey Victorian house in the middle of nowhere.

'Jeddah Creek station, what a magnificent place.'
'Judah, you're looking so well.'

And for the truly brave, *'I miss your parents and I'm sorry for your loss.'*

His brother was somewhere inside, ten years younger and almost a stranger. Reid had been running Jeddah Creek in the four-month gap between their father passing and Judah getting home, and he'd done a good job.

The boy—man—had a strong network of school friends, all freshly graduated and most of them taking a break year before stepping into whatever their families had planned for them. Plenty of Reid's friends were here tonight and he hoped to hell they could hold their liquor because he wasn't exactly policing them. Maybe he should have a word with the exorbitantly priced bar staff the event co-ordinators had insisted on hiring. Let them know that monitoring the alcohol intake of his guests, young and old, was their job, not his.

And then Reid stepped into place at his side, his blue eyes bright and searching.

'She's not here yet. She promised she'd come,' said Reid by way of greeting.

'Who?'

'Bridie.'

There was only one Bridie in Judah's universe and he'd been trying to set up a meeting with her for days. So far, she hadn't even had the courtesy to return his calls. 'Maybe she had a pressing engagement elsewhere.'

'Not Bridie. She's practically a shut-in. Wouldn't leave Devil's Kiss station for years after the incident, and even now she has to work her way up to going out.'

'Then perhaps she's working her way up to it.' The thought of Bridie not making the most of her freedom didn't sit well with him. Stubborn tendrils of anger flickered to life inside him. He'd sacrificed his freedom in service to her. The least she could have done was make the most of her opportunities.

'I know she was worried about how everyone might gossip about her and you,' continued Reid. 'She wasn't looking forward to that part.'

Boo-hoo.

'She's a photographer now,' Reid said next.

He knew.

'Landscapes mostly, of around here. I took her up in the mustering helicopter a month or so back. We ended up taking the door off and rigging up a harness so she could lean out and take aerial shots. I haven't seen them yet, but she said they turned out real good.'

They had.

Resentment curled, a low buzz in the pit of his stomach, and all because his teenage brother was what? Friends with Bridie Starr? Her confidant?

Why hadn't she returned any of his calls?

Bridie was in between him and his brother in age. Twenty-three now, no clueless girl. Would he even recognise her? Of all the photos sent to him these past seven plus years, not one had been of her.

'See that your friends don't drink too much tonight. The last thing we need is an incident.'

'I know. They know. There won't be one.'

How could his teenage brother be so very sure?

Reid seemed to read his mind, and smiled, fierce and swift and just that little bit familiar. 'Your reputation precedes you, man. They'll behave.'

'Does it cause you trouble? My reputation?'

Reid shrugged. 'Not out here.'

'What about when you were at school?'

Another shrug. 'Saved me the trouble of being friends with fair-weather people. That's what Dad used to say.' He squinted towards the east. 'This could be them. Dunno why I expected them to come in the long way around when it's so much quicker to cut across country.'

Judah waited as the thin spiral of dust on the horizon turned into a plume, and a dusty once-white ute came into view. Hard to know what he was feeling, with his emotions locked down so tight, but now was not the time to lose the iron control he'd spent so many years developing.

So what if curiosity was killing him?

So what if the thought of her being a hermit made him seethe?

He could still use that information against her if she didn't bend to his will and sell him back his land. And why wouldn't she sell? She'd done nothing with the land she now owned. It was just sitting there waiting to be reclaimed.

By him.

After all. She owed him.

It took fifteen more minutes before Tom Starr and his daughter walked up the front steps of the homestead and stopped in front of him, and if Judah had thought Bridie astonishingly beautiful before, it was nothing compared to the looks she possessed now. She had a mouth made for crushing, wide-set eyes the colour of cognac, and hair every colour of brown he could imagine—from sun-bleached streaks of honey-gold to burnished bronze shot through with the deepest mahogany. Natural colours, all of them; her hair had been the same wild woodland riot when she was a child.

She still possessed the body of a dancer, all fine bones and elegance, and she carried herself like one too. Her slip of a dress covered her from neck to knee and was a deep twilight blue. No sleeves, no jewellery. Her only accessory was a little black purse that she clutched in front of her body with both hands, her knuckles almost white.

She could barely even look at him.

'Thank you for coming.' His rusty manners had been getting such a workout tonight.

She glanced up, startled, and he found himself enmeshed. Falling into memories he didn't want in his head, and as for allowing them to surface, no. Just no.

'Wouldn't—' She had to stop to clear her throat. 'Wouldn't have missed it. Thank you for inviting us.'

Such pretty lies.

He wanted to reach for the tension knots in his neck. He wanted to reach out and see if her hair felt as silky as it looked.

He wanted to possess this woman who had never been his, who he barely knew but for the fantasies about her that he'd woven in his head. He wanted his father back, an explanation for all the photos she'd sent him month after month, and above all he wanted to know why she'd bought into his birthright. Did she honestly believe he wouldn't be back to claim it?

But what he really wanted—needed—was time out away from her so he could claw back the composure he'd lost the moment she'd locked eyes with him. 'Reid, why don't you show Bridie where she can freshen up and then get her a drink and a plate of food?' Babysit, he might as well have said, but Reid seemed up for the role and Bridie looked grateful.

He watched them go, remembering that at sixteen she'd walked the catwalks of Paris and graced the cover of *Vogue* magazine.

It still showed.

And then he dragged his gaze away from her

retreating figure and prepared to greet her father. 'Tomas.'

'Welcome home,' offered the older man. 'I'm sorry your parents aren't here to greet you.'

'So am I.' He'd never once imagined when he went away that they'd be dead before he returned. 'Maybe you can tell me what happened to my father's business acumen and why he died practically bankrupt.' And why no one had told Judah, and why Tomas had been helping Reid out on the farm in every way he could.

'You sure you want to talk about this here?' Tom Starr didn't look as if he wanted to discuss much at all. 'We could set up a meeting.'

'Been trying to set up a meeting with your daughter all week, Tom. No one's answering and I'm all out of patience.'

The older man looked puzzled. 'Why call Bridie? She doesn't know anything about your father's business dealings.'

But it hadn't been Tom Starr's name on those property deeds, it had been Bridie's. 'What happened to my father?' At least he could get some information from the older man. 'Before he died he let go of things he'd treasured all his life. Cattle bloodlines. Family jewels. *Land.*'

Judah watched as the older man seemed to age another decade before his eyes.

'Grief.' The older man swallowed hard. 'Grief and anger at the way you were treated swallowed your father whole. After you were convicted, your father drank more. So did I and more often than not we drank together. I had plenty of shame to drown and he had a son who'd protected the defenceless and paid an unfair price for it. Your father kept telling me his fancy lawyers would find grounds for appeal, and I just kept on praying it'd happen, but it never did.'

Grounds for appeal. What a joke. As for parole, that concept hadn't worked for him either.

Maybe it had something to do with his swagger.

'A couple of years back I made the mistake of telling your father I was the one who pulled the trigger,' Tom offered gruffly.

Judah stiffened. 'We had a deal. We *swore* that would stay between you and me. No one else.' They'd done it to protect Bridie. So a child would have her only parent at her side to help pick up the pieces of her life. 'You *swore*.'

A man was only as good as his word.

'I thought it would help if he knew you were a hero twice over.'

Some hero. More like a fool. 'Did it?'

'No. He turned even more bitter and twice as uncaring.'

'So who else did you tell? Does Bridie know you pulled that trigger?'

'No one. No one else knows what happened that night. I—after that I thought about it, but—no.'

Why not? He was itching for a fight and he didn't know why. Why did his father get burdened with the truth and not Bridie as well? She was an adult now, wasn't she? No longer that terrified broken child.

'Protect Bridie,' the older man offered weakly. 'She'd take it hard if she knew.'

Protect Bridie. It was the reason he'd shouldered the blame in the first place, all the way to lockup. He'd arrogantly thought his sentence wouldn't be a long one. He'd had the best lawyers money could buy and virtue on his side. He'd never dreamed he'd spend years imprisoned for his supposed sins or that both his parents would be dead before he got out. More fool him.

Protect the innocent children.

How could that be *wrong*?

'My father had hardly any money left when he died. He'd sold off land. You were his friend—or tried to be. What happened?'

'He started playing poker. It was something to do other than stew, I guess. He tried to get me interested, but I'm a lousy poker player and the buy-in was out of my league. Turns out your father wasn't much of a poker player either. I bailed him out of debt a couple of times. I took out a mortgage, but in the end I didn't have any more to give without losing Devil's Kiss. I know he got more money from somewhere, but it wasn't from me.'

There was a ring of truth to the older man's words. 'How much did you give him?'

'None of your business, lad. Give means give. I'm not asking for it back.'

'And you have no idea why your daughter's name is on some of the title deeds for Jeddah Creek station?'

Silence greeted him. A depth of shock that couldn't be feigned. 'I don't know anything about that.'

Interesting.

'Look, I can't say how Bridie got her name on those deeds,' said Tom. 'But at a guess, I'd say she bought them off your father because he had gambling debts to pay that he didn't want your mother to know about. Bridie's not worldly. She doesn't crave power or money or fame, but she does—or did—have money saved from her modelling days and inheritance money from her mother. She doesn't have friends, but she has a good heart, and she owes you, we both do, so please, when you ask her why she holds those deeds hear her out.'

'I would if she'd return my calls.' Hard to believe Tom didn't know about those.

'I know you've left messages for her. I urged her to answer you, but Bridie can take a while to commit to doing things. Fear can paralyse her. And I know people think I mollycoddle her, and maybe I do, but she didn't come back from that night ride whole, Judah, none of us did, and it's been a long road back to even halfway normal for her. She's doing her best here tonight, and she's doing it for you, so don't—'

'Don't what? Turn on her? Take my anger out on her? Why would I do that when I've spent more than seven years *helping you protect her*?'

'I was going to say judge,' the older man said

wearily. 'You're angry because helping us—protecting her—has cost you too much, and I get that. God knows I can never repay you. But don't judge my daughter the way you have every right to judge me.' The other man met his gaze dead on. 'She doesn't have a deceitful bone in her body. You'll see.'

Bridie couldn't seem to stop her hands from shaking. She'd clasped them behind her back in an effort to stop the tremors, but that move exposed the boyish contours of her chest to the gaze of others and she didn't like that either. She'd tried folding her arms in front of her and wrapping her fingers around her upper arms, but that came off as utterly defensive, she knew, and that simply wouldn't do. Holding a drink of any kind was out of the question. Holding someone else's hand might have grounded her but she hadn't done that since her early childhood when she'd held her father's hand or her aunt's hand, or Gert's.

The couple standing next to her started up a conversation about the country they'd flown over to get here, and Bridie joined in, sharing a little local knowledge, and learning in turn that they were from Sydney and the parents of one of Reid's friends. She was then able to talk about Reid's flying lessons and pilot's licence and how they occasionally mustered stock these days using drones rather than helicopters. Reid could fly those too, and so could she.

In ten minutes, she made more small talk than she'd made in six months, but her hands had stopped shaking and her stance didn't feel quite so rigid. She felt almost relaxed. As if she really could mix in with an unknown group of people and do it well.

And then the string group started up and Judah took to the dance floor with a woman old enough to be his grandmother and wealthy enough to wear rings on every finger and pearls at her neck and not give a toss about whether it looked overdone.

The couple beside her took their leave and headed for the dance floor too, such courtly manners for the middle of nowhere, and she wondered whether Reid was up for making a welcome home speech to his brother and whether she'd be called on to say something too. Was that the kind of welcome home she should be considering? Some grand public gesture to cement her allegiance to the man who'd saved her life?

There was no water on the drinks tray a waiter dangled in front of her so she took a champagne and wet her lips and tried not to look like a wallflower in her Givenchy dress and Jimmy Choo shoes, both of them dragged from the bowels of her wardrobe. She'd worn her hair long and had cut bangs into it just before she'd come. Bangs to frame her face and shield her eyes. Eyes she could feel widening as Judah returned his dance partner to the side of an elderly gentleman and locked gazes with her.

His lips tilted into a half-smile as he headed towards her and there was nowhere to run. He didn't ask to take the glass from her hand, he just took it and set it on a nearby table and held out his hand.

'Dance with me.'

It wasn't a question.

She took his hand, hers cold, his warm, and pretended she was back on the catwalks of Paris with all eyes upon her, assessing the clothes and the vision of a celebrated designer. She'd liked modelling beautiful clothes once upon a time. She'd loved strutting her stuff on the catwalk, fluid and assured, pretending she was a dancer or Audrey Hepburn or Coco Chanel. Pretending she was someone special. That particular flight of fantasy got her to the dance floor, small mercies, only now she had another problem as Judah turned towards her and put his palm to her waist.

'I can't waltz,' she whispered, panicked. For all that Gert said her father had been quite the dancer in his day, he'd certainly never taken the time to teach his daughter that particular skill. 'I never learned.'

'Then we'll sway from side to side like half the other couples on the floor. I don't care.' He drew her in and the scent of eucalyptus and something altogether masculine drifted with him. 'Put your hand on my upper arm.' He kept gentle hold of her other hand and she did as suggested, and his arm was warm too, beneath the fine fabric of his suit.

She squeezed just a little bit and he raised a wicked eyebrow in return. She was used to wiry men with plenty of muscle and not a lot of fat to be going on with, but Judah was built to a whole different level. 'What have they been feeding you?'

'Slop.'

He probably wasn't joking. 'Sorry, I—stupid comment. The food tonight is excellent.'

'You haven't eaten any.'

How did he know? 'Well, it looks good.'

'So do you.' Words that made his lips curl in a whole different way from before, and if that was a smile, heaven help him. 'But you already know that.'

'I do know that. I dressed up in my best because I wanted to make sure I honoured your welcome home party by looking as put together as I can.' She followed his dance lead, stepping slowly side to side, and fixed her gaze over his shoulder.

He added a slow turn to their swaying. 'I liked the photos you sent.'

One a month, every month, since he'd gone away. She felt his gaze on her face but refused to look at him. 'The first ones weren't very good.'

She could feel his shrug. 'They were to me.'

'I almost stopped sending them. You never wrote back.'

'What would you have had me say?'

And there was another question she had no answer to, but the music kept playing and their feet kept moving and maybe they didn't need to say anything. She'd shown her face and accepted his command to dance—as if she'd had a choice—and she felt as if she held lightning and thunder in her arms. Why wouldn't she feel that way? He was her ultimate protector and he'd paid mightily for taking on that role, sacrificing his freedom so she could survive hers.

'You haven't answered any of my calls,' he said.

'I…know.'

'Too busy or too afraid of me?'

Another question she didn't know how to answer without throwing every vulnerability she owned at his feet for him to tread on. She spared him a glance. Those eyes…some kind of mossy green, ringed with such a dark navy-grey around the edges. She'd always thought him fierce on account of those eyes. A force to be reckoned with and a perfect match for wild Jeddah Creek station.

He'd killed a man who'd been stalking her. Pulled her bound and shaking from the cramped, pitch-black car boot she'd been trapped in and delivered her safely into the arms of her father. He'd been locked away because of it, and she owed him her truth.

'At first I was afraid of everything and everyone. Shadows made me jump. Other people made me cringe. I could barely leave my room. And then one day my father yelled at me from the other side of my bedroom door. He said, "Judah's the one sitting in a prison room staring at the walls, Bridie, not you. How do you think he'd feel about squandering his freedom on someone who's refusing to live?"'

'Smart man, your father.'

She couldn't look away from him. 'A week later I went to the kitchen for breakfast. A few weeks after that I made it to the back door and stepped out onto the veranda. I took a picture and sent it to you.' She'd kept right on sending them. 'For seven years, six months and two days I've thought of you sacrificing your freedom for my life. It made me step out of my comfort zone and keep on walking. So, am I afraid of you? No. But I have been using you for years as a cattle prod to help me face my fears. My feelings for you are complicated.'

'I'll say,' he muttered, after a very long stretch of silence.

She had nothing more to say. Nothing to do except fidget beneath that watchful, wary gaze.

'What are you going to do now you've lost your cattle prod?'

'Do you always ask such difficult questions?'

He shrugged. 'I don't usually ask personal questions at all. Like you said, whatever is between us is complicated.'

She looked around the glittering ballroom filled with Australia's beautiful and wealthy and wondered if any of them walked with fear as a constant companion, like her. Or which of them had broken the law and paid the price, like Judah, and how hard they'd had to fight to come back from that. 'I'm glad you're back. I didn't answer your calls because I wanted to tell you in person. *Thank you* in person for saving me.'

She felt the tension in him rather than saw it. A simmering waiting quality that burned. A heavy-lidded gaze that banked hard, but not before she'd seen the sudden flame of sexual interest in his eyes. Oh, she'd seen that before, but not from him, never from him.

And she might not be afraid of him, but she *was* afraid of what could happen to a man with too much pent-up desire and not nearly enough self-control. They lost their minds and let fantasy rule. They saw only what they wanted to.

And then Judah loosened his hold and stepped back, and suddenly she could breathe again, even if her hands were too clammy and her body too hot.

'My father sold you land in the last year of his life. Yes or no?'

'Yes.' She'd been dreading this part of the conversation. 'It's complicated. The money didn't always go directly to him. Sometimes I paid bills for him instead.'

'You mean gambling debts.'

'I didn't ask. But, yes, probably.'

'I want that land back. Whatever you paid, I'll pay it. More, if that's what you want.'

'No, you don't understand.'

'Double the price you paid. I want it back.'

'Judah, you don't understand. It's not for sale. You can—'

'Everyone, if I may have your attention.' His voice rang out across the ballroom, stopping music and movement and turning all eyes towards them. His arm at her waist was a band of steel, keeping her in place, but why? What was he doing?

'First, I'd like to welcome you all here tonight. I

appreciate the time and trouble so many of you have taken to get here. Welcome to Jeddah Creek station. I hope you find the hospitality and the connections you make here tonight to your liking.'

A waiter approached them with a tray full of drinks and he took one and passed it to her before collecting another for himself. 'Secondly, I'd like to introduce one particular woman to you all. A woman whose name you will have no doubt heard in connection with mine even if you haven't met her personally. A woman of rare compassion and resilience. Someone who has seen the darkest actions mankind has to offer and yet somehow manages to retain her sanity and goodness.'

He couldn't possibly be talking about her.

'Someone who inspired me to look outward rather than in, at a time when all I could see were concrete walls and prison bars. A pioneering soul, with a vision for merging two great farming families and two iconic properties to allow for more conservation projects and forward management of the land we hold so dear. Ladies and gentlemen, please raise your glasses to Bridie Starr.' He smiled down at her, all shark. 'My future wife.'

Say *what*, now?

Wife? What wife? Had he lost his mind while in prison? A little bit of insanity to accompany that very impressive, very fine physique?

'Smile,' he ordered softly, as the guests applauded, and showed her how to do it. 'People will take one look at you and think we're not serious.' He touched the rim of his glass to hers. Just that little bit lower than the rim of her glass, to be precise, and wasn't that supposed to indicate some measure of respect? 'To us.'

'What us?' she hissed behind the cover of golden bubbles. 'What exactly do you think you're doing?'

'Getting my land back.'

'By *marrying* me?' She laughed. She couldn't help it. She was still laughing as she lifted the glass to her lips and proceeded to drain it. Moments later a waiter had whisked it away and they were dancing again, her mind a whirl and her body following along behind. 'Can you be *any* more insulting?'

'You refused to sell. What did you think I would do?'

'Oh, I don't know. You could have waited two more seconds and *listened* to what I had to say. You could have easily done that, but no, straight to blackmail and coercion and *marriage*? Are you *nuts*?' She stepped in close, super aware of all the people beginning to move around them as she raised her lips to his ear. 'The only reason I bought the land in the first place was because I didn't want your father selling it to anyone else. I kept it safe from harm so I could return it to you, because I *owe* you.' She took a deep breath and let the true depth of her anger show. 'I was two seconds away from *giving it to you*. You utter *idiot*.'

CHAPTER TWO

IF JUDAH HAD learned anything in lockup it was to never back down, even if you had just picked the wrong fight. That mindset had got him through more than seven years of prison politics alive and relatively unscathed. Whether it would get him through the rest of this dance remained to be seen.

'We don't have to stay engaged for long,' he tried, and she trod on his toe with the point of a scissor-tipped stiletto. 'Ow.'

'You're absolutely right.' Her eyes glowed like cognac. 'Five minutes should do it.'

But he couldn't break their engagement five minutes after announcing it. He had a reputation to protect. Status that relied on money, hype and his willingness to kill to protect the innocent. Foolishness could never be part of that mix. 'One month, and I'll make it worth your while. Diamonds. A carat a day.'

'And now he thinks I can be bought…'

Everyone has a price.

'I'll pay triple whatever you paid for my land in the first place.'

'Really not motivated by money...'

What was she motivated by? Had she mentioned anything he could use? Anything at all? 'Ah, but think of the privacy you can buy with it. I hear the Conrad place might be coming on the market soon.' The Conrads were their current neighbours to her north.

She eyed him sharply. 'Who told you that?'

'The Conrads. Look, the only reason I went with the marriage plan in the first place was because I never dreamed you'd be so stup—'

'*Do* keep going,' she murmured dulcetly. 'Dig that hole deep.'

'I never dreamed you'd be so *generous* as to *give* the land back.' Where was the grift in that? The jockeying for every tiny advantage? 'You realise all this could have been avoided if you'd taken my calls?' Ouch. Ow! So much for fancy butter-soft-leather dress shoes. 'Do you know how sharp your shoes are?'

Although not as sharp as her tongue.

In prison, he'd been Mr No Feelings at All.

Ten minutes after clapping eyes on Bridie and a tsunami of emotions was threatening to overwhelm him. Anger, desire, yearning, embarrassment, frustration and more desire—all of it itching to escape him no matter how many other people here tonight would see and use his weakness against him.

For years and years and far too many *years* he'd been waiting for the day when he could come home to Jeddah Creek and put his life back together and build on the legacy his family had left him. He'd make his parents and his brother proud. He'd restore the family name he'd dragged through the dust. He'd become a philanthropic force to be reckoned with.

Instead, here he was, ten days out and about and making an utter fool of himself.

'Don't do anything rash. Avoid split-second decisions.'

Too late for that.

'Give others the benefit of the doubt.'

Missed that one too, even with Tom Starr's blatant plea to do just that.

All he'd sensed was her resistance to selling the land that should have been his and he'd been back in the prison yard, fighting to win.

How could he be so stupid as to let her get under his skin?

It was too hot in this ballroom full of expensively dressed predators.

And what was this wave of cold sweeping over him like nothing he'd felt before? Not when he'd stood before the court, waiting for his sentence to be handed down. Not when he'd tried to stem a dead man's wounds and bathed his hands in blood.

He didn't realise he'd stopped moving until Bridie stepped from his arm and tugged at his hand.

'Come on,' she muttered. 'We've danced enough.'

And then they were leaving the dance floor and heading for the nearest exit, and he did not have control—couldn't even breathe for the iron band around his chest. All he could do was hold on and hope she knew where she was going.

'Blake.'

Devlin Conrad stood in their way, his wife Judith at his side, and both of them were beaming.

'Please, may we be the first to congratulate you on your engagement?' said Judith. 'What a wonderful union. It makes so much sense. And your land-care initiative is music to our ears.' She glanced towards her husband. 'If you added our property into that mix, just imagine what you could do.'

Devlin Conrad nodded. 'We should talk about that.'

He could only nod.

'Are you looking to sell?' asked Bridie.

'Yes, but not to just anyone. To you both. To make our run part of your vision.'

'Done.' How he squeezed the word out he'd never know. But it took the last of his air.

'Yes,' said Bridie quickly. 'We'll be in touch. So sorry, excuse us, we forgot the ring.'

She led him to the veranda and then to the left, around the corner, trying the handle on every door. He'd never noticed before how evenly spaced they were and how much they reminded him of institutional corridors.

At last she found an unlocked door and pulled him in, shutting the door behind them and pushing him against the wall with a surprisingly firm hand. They

were in the old stone laundry and the only light came
from the slatted shutters high above the door, and
with the dark, enclosed space came a fresh panic that
had nothing and everything to do with being a fool.

'Breathe,' she demanded, and he would. Soon.

Just as soon as he got out of this cell.

'You're having a panic attack.'

This time it was his turn to lead her through an
interior door and into a long lit hallway. Was he blue
yet from all the breathing he wasn't doing?

He needed space.

Space and quiet and no people tracking his weakness and waiting for a chance to come at him.

The formal sitting room was at the end of the
hall, with its dark jarrah wainscoting and parque-
try floor, its pressed tin ceiling and deep blue walls
and expanse enough to swing a cow. It also housed
several of the most uncomfortable Jacobean needle-
point armchairs in the world, a couple of ancestral
portraits and a dusty collection of stuffed hawks.

It was still better than the little concrete laundry.

This time Bridie had the forethought to switch
on the light beside the door. Her action lit a naked
globe hanging from a long cord in the far corner
of the room. There were other switches, other light
sources in the room. That one had been left in place
to please historians.

'Shall I shut the door or leave it open?' she asked.

'Leave it.' He didn't close doors these days, not
one in all the time he'd been home.

'Still not breathing,' she reminded him, and he vowed to get right on that. Might as well hang onto the back of a chair while he was at it, in the interest of staying upright.

Breathe, you scum.

Can't you even do that right?

Breathe.

Bridie walked around the edges of the room, turning table lamps and feature lights on until it was lit up like some kind of mad night at the museum, and he tracked her every step.

There'd been no stuffed birds in prison. Heaven knew it was an odd thought to be having, but he held to it and somehow it reassured him. Breathing resumed. Bridie kept paying him no attention.

'Who's the stuffed hawk collector?' she wanted to know.

'My great-grandfather. The one in the portrait over the fireplace.' The one who'd come to Australia but had never ever managed to call Jeddah Creek station home. A failure, they'd called him. Too pampered for the outback. Soft in the head.

But he *had* stayed the course and built the family wealth for the next generation of Blakes to inherit. Only with his burial back in England had he finally returned home.

Bridie continued her leisurely lap of the room and stopped in front of the portrait. 'It says here his name was Edward. Very noble.'

'It wasn't a panic attack.'

She stood there looking like an angel in the glow of a butter-yellow lamp as she turned to study a John Constable painting of the English countryside. 'I used to get them a lot,' she said quietly. 'Panic attacks. I thought I recognised the signs. Not that it matters—I needed to get away from the crowd before I had a meltdown too.'

'It wasn't a meltdown.'

''Course not.' She slanted him a look from beneath impossibly long lashes and he promptly lost what little breath he'd managed to scrape together. 'I needed to leave the ballroom. I thought I was serving your needs as well.'

His need was blindingly clear.

This wasn't a prison yard. Bridie hadn't been looking to screw him over. She'd had no beef with him at all, although she probably did *now*. He needed to apologise.

'I'm sorry.' Those words came easier than expected. 'I overreacted when you said you weren't selling the land. I didn't let you finish. I didn't listen and I put you in a bad position.'

He shoved his hands in his pockets and stared at a stuffed goshawk, with its delicately striped breast feathers and sharp yellow eyes.

How a dead bird's glare could shame him into wanting to be a better man he did not know, but that was exactly what it was doing. Or maybe it was the undeniable goodness of the woman who stood quietly in the shadows. Giving him space. Doing her level best to see to his needs.

'I can make another public statement later this evening and break the engagement,' he offered. 'You don't have to be there. People can think what they want.'

Another rash, split-second decision.

Just what he needed.

Bridie trailed her fingers lightly across the carvings on the back of a chair. 'What about the Conrads' offer?'

He'd barely registered that. But he did want their land and he hoped to hell they'd still be interested in selling it to him once he'd called the engagement off.

'I mean, it's not as if you don't have the money,' she continued quietly. 'But they mostly seemed interested in selling it not just to you but to *us*.'

There was that.

'I'd like to hear about your conservation plans too,' she murmured.

He stared.

'And I'm thinking that if we stayed engaged for a while we could both save some face. You could buy the Conrad place, and I could have a fiancé for when I'm in Sydney next. That'd be good.'

She was doing a better job than he was of planning their way out of this mess. 'What's in Sydney?'

'A gallery exhibition of some of my landscape photographs. Part of the agreement is that I be there in person on opening night. You could come too and be my…' Her words tailed off as if she didn't know how to finish that sentence.

'Cattle prod?' he offered.

'That too. You can be my notorious muse if you like. I'm sure the gallery's publicist would be thrilled.'

'When's it on?' He hadn't left Jeddah Station since leaving the correctional centre. Given tonight's performance in public, that was probably a good thing. Was he ready for Sydney? He didn't know. But if he didn't go he'd never know. 'When's your exhibition?'

'Two weeks this coming Thursday. The gallery is at The Rocks and I'm staying at the Ocean View, near the bridge. I'll book another room for you; we wouldn't have to share.'

The thought of sharing a room with her brought forth a whole new set of problems he didn't want to admit to. 'I can do that.' His need to negotiate and control what was happening took hold. 'In return we commit to one month's fake engagement.'

'There's more.'

'More gallery openings?'

'More that I want from you in return for committing to this fake engagement.'

He spread his hands and waited.

She took a deep breath. 'Reid's been talking about building some eco lodges up on the ridges between Jeddah Creek and Devil's Kiss. He wants to bring tourists in. Give them a taste of red dirt and endless skies. Helicopter rides. Quad bike tours. I hate the idea but if it's going to happen, I want to be part of it. Financial investment, a voice when it comes to what type of tourists to target, the lot. It's not that I don't trust Reid, but he's young—'

'And you're not?'

'And enthusiastic,' she continued doggedly. 'And you're talking about putting strangers on my doorstep, and privacy and safety is a huge concern for me. I want a say in how it's done.'

He had no idea what she was talking about. His little brother hadn't yet seen fit to mention those plans. 'I can't promise anything without Reid's input.'

'He looks up to you. He'll follow your lead.'

Judah sincerely hoped not. 'If he does agree to involve you, we can announce the deal when we break our engagement. Better as business partners and so on. And for that I want three months' worth of fake engagement to you.' Having a temporary fiancée might even help bring others on board with his not-for-profit conservation trust plans. Investors loved a settled man.

'Agreed.'

For someone so seemingly fragile, she certainly knew how to combat coercion, intimidation and fake engagement announcements. She was making him feel like an amateur.

'Breathing back to normal now? That band around your chest loosening up? Chills gone?'

How did she—? Goddamn panic attack symptoms. 'Yes.'

'Great, because Reid and my father are standing in the doorway and I think they want a word with us.'

Great. Just great. How much had they heard?

He turned, squared his shoulders, and prepared for the worst.

'Interesting announcement,' said Reid. 'A little warning would have been good.'

'Spur of the moment,' he offered. *Give* him his land back after buying it fair and square. Who *did* that?

'We'd been talking about land mergers and conservation options and business deals and when the Conrads started talking about selling we might have got a little carried away,' said Bridie.

Reid ran a hand across the back of his neck as if working out the kinks. 'So is your engagement like a fake one to get people on board, or some kind of business merger, or are we talking the real thing?'

'It's real enough,' said Judah and stared his brother and her father down. 'Any objections?'

'I'm good.' Reid shared a glance with Tom. 'I'm also going to go find sane people to drink with now. And, uh, good luck.'

Reid left. Tom stayed. The older man looked from one of them to the other and back again, finally settling his shuttered gaze on Judah. 'She'll forgive you anything. You should know this.'

'No, Dad, not anything,' corrected Bridie. 'But I don't think Judah's beyond repair. You don't think he's beyond repair either—you've praised him often enough over the years, remember?'

And why shouldn't he have Tom Starr's approval? Judah wanted to roar.

That night...that crazy, bloated clusterfest of a night that had branded Judah a killer and Tom a grateful father still haunted them all. Would they ever be free of it?

Until this moment he hadn't truly understood that the answer was *no*. The lie at the heart of it would never let him and Tom Starr go. 'Good to know I'm not *beyond repair*.'

'Hey, no, wait. Repair was my word,' Bridie said hurriedly. 'And definitely the wrong word. Dad, I know the engagement announcement surprised you and you want answers. And I'm not going to insult your intelligence by claiming it wasn't a bit spur of the moment. It's probably not going to last, but while we're on a roll why not explore what we might be able to do conservation-wise if we were to combine Jeddah Creek, Devil's Kiss and Talulah Sky? Think about it.'

'If he hurts you—

'Dad, I'm not sixteen any more. I'm not so naive I can't see the make of a person or whether they're out to harm me. I'm not being taken advantage of. I'm not doing anything I don't want to do, and Judah's not out to harm me.'

Judah and her father locked gazes.

They both knew what happened to people who chose to harm Bridie.

'Let me know when you want to leave,' said Tom. 'I'm ready whenever you are.'

'Half an hour,' she said.

'Half an hour,' echoed her father and left, as if he couldn't stand watching them a moment longer.

'How are you tracking?' she asked when they were alone again, and the honest answer was not well. He kept waiting for retaliation and instead he got fragile little Bridie doing her best to soothe him, humour him and, heaven help them all, *protect* him.

This was not how his world should be.

'Getting there,' he muttered. What else could he say? *Take me back to lockup where I know how the world works?*

He crossed to a painting of wolfhounds racing across a field of green and lifted the painting from its hook to reveal a safe—one of several in the house, but this one housed some of the family's older, finer jewels. Or, given his father's gambling habit, maybe it now held the paste equivalent.

'You need a ring. Come and look.' He gestured her over and opened velvet box after velvet box of jewellery. The diamond and emerald tennis bracelet looked sparkly enough and he opened the clasp. 'Give me your wrist.'

Bridie held out her wrist and he fastened it and thought of the zip ties they used on prisoners and hoped to hell she didn't feel similarly tied down. At least her wrists weren't bound together. 'My grandmother had a diamond and emerald ring that should be in here somewhere. The emerald is the centre stone with two diamonds either side and she had slender hands like you.'

A dozen different rings of various shapes and sizes later, he found the one he was looking for and eased it from its snowy velvet cradle.

There was something timeless about it. The emerald a rich and vivid green that held its own against the diamonds that flanked it, all of it set in filigree white gold.

'Oh, wow,' she said. 'Art deco.'

'Yes or no?'

'Oh, yes.'

She held out her hand. He slid the ring on her finger and it fit as if it had been made for her.

She watched it sparkle for a time and then nodded. 'Beautiful. I'll give it back when we're done.'

'Keep it. When we finish up you should keep it.'

She looked startled. 'I couldn't. It's a family ring, isn't it?'

Why was she so surprised by his generosity when hers had humbled and shamed him? 'And now it's yours.'

Their re-entry into the ballroom brought on a torrent of congratulations and well wishes.

What would he do next, people with bright smiles wanted to know, and then didn't know what to do when he said give back to his community, restore his family name and preserve the land in his care.

Congratulations on your engagement, they said. What a fairy-tale ending for you both.

Let me know when you want to do business, they said, as if he were a goose fat with golden eggs.

Bridie too had to weather a swollen river of effusive comments.

'Look at you, all grown up and so beautiful.' That seemed to be the general verdict and she wore the comment awkwardly.

'I can't help the way I look,' she murmured to him after one such comment. 'It's not exactly a skill.'

'What a catch you've made,' others said to her in his presence. 'A lord of the realm, fiercely protective and money to burn. Lucky *you*.'

Her hands had begun to shake again.

Maybe it was his turn to rescue her. 'Time's up,' he told her. 'Let's find your father and get you out of here.'

She didn't protest. She did lean over and press her lips to the edge of his mouth in farewell, and it would have taken only the tiniest turn of his head to light a fire he'd have no hope of ever putting out.

'Talk soon,' she said, and he gave the tiniest nod because her scent was in the air and words were beyond him again. 'I want to know which photos of mine you liked best. Make me a pile and once all your visitors have gone I'll show you where I took every one of them. A welcome home trip.'

'You'd do that?'

'Of course I will.' She stood too close. It had been so long since he'd held a woman in his arms, any woman, let alone one who could make his head swim. His control was stretched so very thin. 'It's just kindness.'

Judah returned to his guests and followed his original plan for the evening to make himself available. He drank sparingly and listened to business plans and politicking. He took note of relationships and the levers that sustained them. He filed away every last sniff of information he collected and made no promises whatsoever when it came to what he intended to do with his money. He was back in touch with the movers and shakers of this world and he fully intended to carve out his place in it, but it would be on his terms, not theirs. By the end of the evening the smarter ones had figured as much, and the rest... they'd learn.

When the party wound down and people went back to their luxury planes and had their pilots take them away, or slept in their planes, or stayed on in his guest rooms, Judah took a farm ute and headed north, away from all the people, until he reached a stand of old red river gums with their distinctive bark peeling back to a smooth and ghostly white.

He spread out his swag in the bed of the ute, with the tailgate down and the vast sky above. Thin mattress, canvas cover, and a pillow so soft he could hardly bear the comparison to the prison lump he was used to. He wondered if his brother would suggest he get therapy if he made this his bed for the foreseeable future.

No walls. Just stars.

No other people breathing, snoring or weeping. He'd swapped those sounds for the thrumming of riverbank insects going about their business.

This place. Photo number sixty-two of the eighty-eight photos Bridie had sent to him over the years—he'd memorised each one before carefully handing them back across the desk to be put with the rest of the belongings he'd been stripped of.

She had no idea how much her photos had meant to him, those monthly reminders of who he was and where he belonged.

He'd had no idea how closely they might have documented her steps these past years. From the safety of her back door to the edge of the veranda. From the old Hills Hoist hung with freshly washed clothes to the edge of the house paddock and the windmill and water trough. Such familiar things, each one set just that little bit further from her homestead.

He wasn't the only one to have lost years of freedom because of the actions of a thwarted madman—he knew that now.

In his absence, she'd built him up to be someone he wasn't, but he'd done exactly the same to her. They needed to move past that if they wanted to be business and land conservation partners. He'd agreed to that, heaven help him. Same way he'd agreed to be her fiancé for the next three months. He who had no business whatsoever being around someone so delicate and beautiful. Someone who could unravel him just by looking in his direction. Someone who could make him forget where he was with the touch of her hand.

He missed intimacy so much and she was right there…ready to forgive him anything. Thinking of him as some kind of hero—and what a joke that was, even if thinking of himself as a hero had made his incarceration that much easier to bear. Protector of the innocent, no matter the cost. Honourable to the end. A man of his word.

A *good* man.

Until tonight, when he'd ripped that myth apart.

Forcing an unwanted engagement on Bridie. Lying about it to his brother and her father and everyone else in order to save face and belatedly offer Bridie what protection he could. Pledging to buy Conrad land under false pretences. Wanting to take Bridie's sweet, parting kiss and turn it into an inferno.

Not exactly a good man any more, was he?

'Don't do anything rash. Avoid split-second decisions.'

'Give yourself time to adjust.'

'Give others the benefit of the doubt.'

He'd done *none* of that and Bridie had paid the price with an engagement she couldn't possibly want. He'd allowed Bridie to protect *him* when he'd fallen apart, and that couldn't happen again. He needed to undo all the tics he'd learned in prison and figure out who he was and who he wanted to be, and above all keep his desire for Bridie's touch to himself and *not* take advantage of her goodwill and sweet nature and sense of obligation.

Pull yourself together, Judah, don't be a disgrace.

Be a better man.

Rather than be ashamed.

CHAPTER THREE

'WHERE'VE YOU BEEN?'

Judah halted at the question his brother threw at him from his position behind the kitchen counter. A large cooktop and a couple of ovens lined the wall behind his brother, with a cool room at one end and a regular fridge at the other. Odd, how such a seemingly innocent question might grate on a man who'd been forced to account for every minute of his day for such a long time. Or maybe not so odd at all.

'Because I made a heap of breakfast for the guys before they left and I saved you some. So what'll it be?' his brother continued, oblivious to Judah's scowl. 'The works? Bacon, sausages, tomato, scrambled eggs, toast. Or there's the veggo option of bruschetta. I didn't make that one. Nico's training to be a chef.'

'And Nico is…?'

'A friend from school. Trent Nicholson. Good man.'

He should probably stop thinking of his brother and all his friends as boys. He should also stop being so quick to take offence. Soon would be good. Making some kind of decision about what to eat for breakfast would be good too. *Any time now, slow-poke, you can do it.* He doubted the prison psych's advice to take his time when making decisions applied to something as simple as food choice. 'I'll take the second one.'

'Coffee too?'

'You're speaking my language.'

Reid beamed and set about getting the fancy machine to produce liquid heaven, and Judah finally forgave him that very first 'where've you been?'. 'You said your friends have already gone?' The city caterers were still around, he'd seen them on his way in, but they too were scheduled to leave by lunch-time. Solitude again.

'Yeah. Couple of them could have stayed on, but I didn't know how you'd feel about that. You were pretty clear about wanting everyone gone by this morning.'

'That didn't include your school friends. This is your home too.' Clearly, they had some work to do when it came to communicating wants and needs.

Reid slung food and coffee in front of him and Judah pulled up a stool and tucked in, still silently marvelling at the taste of good food. Not to mention he now had unlimited access to all kinds of kitchen utensils that could so easily be shaped into shivs. Not that he needed to shape anything into a shiv, given that a row of kitchen knives was right there behind his brother, stuck to a magnetic strip on the wall.

His brother followed Judah's gaze. 'You keep looking at them. Why?'

Probably not a good idea to mention that he was counting them. Again. And that he counted them every time he walked into the room to make sure they were all still there.

'They can go in a drawer if you like.'

'Then I'd have to open the drawer to count them and that'd be worse.'

Reid had his mouth open and his fork loaded but everything stopped at Judah's gravelly confession.

'I see,' he offered quietly, and then slowly filled his mouth with food.

Judah tried to see any trace of his freckle-faced eleven-year-old brother in the quiet eighteen-year-old stranger sitting across from him and could find none. Reid was whipcord lean, tanned and a recent haircut had gone some way towards taming his thick, wavy brown hair. His blue eyes were still as bright as Judah remembered, except laughter had been replaced by a wariness usually reserved for freshwater crocs.

'I expect it'll take a while for you to adapt,' his little brother said carefully. 'I had some calls from a social worker before you got out. She gave me a bit of a rundown on what to expect.'

'What did she tell you?'

'Are you feeling angry, frustrated and depressed yet?'

'Not yet.'

'Good start.' Reid nodded encouragingly, and

for some reason Judah wanted to laugh. 'Anything changed so much you barely recognise it?'

'Apart from you? No.'

'Do you feel overwhelmed?'

Last night didn't count. 'No.'

'Any negative influences I should know about?'

'I had a run-in with a horsefly yesterday and won. I'll try not to hang around them too often.'

'Good luck with that out here. Any addictions?'

'Not yet. And I doubt I'm going to become addicted to your breakfast conversation.'

'Har har. I'm checking in with you like they told me to. Guess you pass the test.' Reid nodded his approval. 'You want to come flying with me today? I can show you the new access road and set of yards we put in up near Pepper Tree Ridge.'

'You could.'

'We could pick Bridie up on the way. She likes it up there.'

Why wouldn't Reid and Bridie get together every now and then and have formed a friendship born of common ground and neighbourliness? Why did he scowl at the thought of it? 'I'd rather we didn't include Bridie. Not today.'

'Trouble in engagement land already?'

'No.' How much should he confess? But the thought of looking like a weakling idiot in front of his brother didn't sit well with him. He was the *older* brother, dammit. 'But it's not exactly a traditional engagement and I like a bit of distance.'

'I'll say,' muttered Reid and narrowed his gaze. 'Do you blame her?'

'For what?'

'For getting kidnapped and you having to sully your soul and kill a man in order to get her back?' Reid had a frown on his face.

'Do I blame Bridie for my sullied soul? No.' He didn't *have* a sullied soul. Not yet, and he aimed to keep it that way.

For the first five years of his incarceration he'd stuck steadfastly to the idea that it was nothing more than his *duty* to protect the weakest link in his world. Damn right he could still look at himself in the mirror and know he'd done the right thing.

His resolve had faltered somewhere around the seven-year mark when his mother died.

When his father had followed not two months later, passing so swiftly they hadn't even been able to arrange prison leave for Judah to say goodbye, Judah's resolve had faltered some more.

He'd missed so much. Left his parents alone out here, then left Reid to fend for himself. Reid, who for these past six months had been in charge of thirty-odd thousand square kilometres of some of the most dangerous and inhospitable grazing land in Australia. A property Reid didn't even have a claim to because Judah as firstborn son had inherited the lot. But not one scrap of that was Bridie's doing or Bridie's fault. 'I don't blame Bridie for any of that. My actions, my responsibility.'

'Hero.'

'In your dreams.'

'Yep. Big hero.'

'You keep thinking like that and I'll only disappoint you. I don't want to disappoint you, Reid. I want to get to know you and for you to know me.'

A sentiment that silenced his brother completely.

'Bridie mentioned last night about you wanting to build tourist lodges up on the ridges,' Judah continued carefully. 'Care to share?'

His brother nodded, his eyes brightening. 'I want to build a couple of luxury eco-tourism lodges up above river bend. Fly-in fly-out, a minimum five-day package, with fishing, sunset cookouts, stargazing, sunrise wellness yoga or something, I don't know, and day trips out to Carper's Ridge. This is my home and I love it, but it's lonely, and that won't change unless we change it, you know?'

'Or you could move to where the people are.'

Reid held his gaze. 'Is that what you want me to do? Go? Firstborn takes all when it comes to land, I know that. And I can set down elsewhere if you want me gone. But you asked me what I want, so I'm telling you. I want to stay here. I want to fly interesting people around and find out how this place inspires them. I want a home of my own, one day, on Jeddah Creek land or nearby, and if you buy the Conrad place, maybe I could go there. Eventually or something.'

'Definitely.'

'Yes!' Reid flung his arms in the air and did a lap of the kitchen island, every inch the teenager. 'Yes! My hero.' Reid came at him from behind, wrapping his long arms around him and kissing him on the side of the head. Whatever discomfort with physical contact Judah had with people, Reid clearly hadn't inherited it.

'Don't make me lunge for the kitchen knives, man,' Judah protested. 'Get off me.'

'I love you.' Hug. 'My brother the land baron.' Kiss.

'Okay, that's enough.'

'Mate, we need to work on your people skills,' said Reid, returning to his side of the counter, thank God. He was like an overgrown puppy. 'But apart from you buying all the land, and me wanting in on that deal in any way I can, what do you think of my eco-tourism idea?'

'Would you like a silent, cashed-up brother for a partner?'

'Hell, yes.'

'What about a concerned neighbour for a partner? One who wants a say in how things will be run?'

'Tom?'

'Bridie.'

Reid frowned and scratched his head. 'Bridie wouldn't be silent.'

His take as well. 'Correct. But if we're going to have a tourist area we need a development plan. Set limits that won't be crossed and have happy neighbours, Bridie in particular, and make sure she doesn't feel threatened by you bringing strangers onto their land.'

'You're protecting her,' said Reid with a sigh.

'Would you prefer I didn't?'

'No.' Reid scratched his hair and left a peacock's ruffle in the dark mess. 'Or yes. Maybe I want her to push on more than she does.' He shrugged. 'Maybe we can do three lodges. One for your use, one for mine, one for Bridie and her photography. She could run courses. Teach.'

'Or maybe she won't be into that at all,' Judah warned. 'But you could ask.'

Reid nodded. 'Or you could.'

'Silent partner, remember?'

'Not so silent now though, are you?'

'Set a business up to serve a need and it'll grow. And, yeah.' He'd been thinking about conservation management plans for years and he liked where his brother's head was at. 'Maybe not so silent after all.'

Bridie couldn't quite comprehend what her father was saying. Possibly because he was saying very little.

'I'm heading off for a while.' That had been his first sentence, swiftly followed by, 'Don't expect me back any time soon.'

'But where are you going?' She followed him out to his twin cab as he tossed an old-fashioned suit-case in the back. The vehicle was old enough to need new shock absorbers and back brakes and probably a couple of tyres. Serviceable enough when driving around the ten thousand or so square miles they called Devil's Kiss, but beyond that he was pushing his luck.

'But where are you going?' she asked again when he didn't respond.

'Might go and see your aunt for a while.'

'In the Kimberleys?' Because that was where Aunt Beth lived, and as well as needing a reliable vehicle to get there, even a one-way trip was likely to take days. Her father had never once left her here alone for days. 'Is she sick?'

He shrugged, squirrelly and unable to meet her gaze.

'Are *you* sick?' Although, if he was, surely he'd be heading east for medical care rather than west.

'No. I just need to get away from here for a while. Maybe a long while.'

And then he pulled her close, kissed her cheek, muttered, 'Take care of yourself, love,' and was gone in a cloud of dust that would linger for half an hour before settling.

She stood alone, hands on hips, in front of the white wooden homestead, a few carefully tended gum trees flanking it, and watched him go with a sinking feeling she hadn't felt in years.

Not as if he were leaving her unprotected.

She was a perfectly healthy twenty-three-year-old, born and raised on Devil's Kiss remote cattle station and perfectly comfortable around spiders, snakes, reptiles, feral pigs and uncivilised bulls. She knew every bit of this land and the people on it.

Curtis and his elderly partner, Maria, lived in the station-hand house—retired now and living rent free in exchange for the safety of their company and a few odd jobs here and there.

Jake and Cobb were salaried cattlemen and they and their wives and children lived in newer cottages further north and closer to town. She could call on them at any time if anything that she couldn't do needed doing.

She had Gert for three days every fortnight, and Gert even had a room in the house. It wasn't as if Bridie was being abandoned in the middle of nowhere.

Shucking her boots at the door—because why undo all of Gert's hard work?—she stepped into the kitchen area of the grand old homestead that glittered like a shimmery jewel in a desert of burnt umber. It was a one-storey house, not nearly as big as the Blake place, but similarly Victorian flavoured. It had a corrugated-iron roof and wraparound verandas framed by elaborate wrought-iron lacework. Stone walls kept the inside of the house reasonably cool and the windows and abundance of French doors leading onto the verandas let in light, but not sunshine, and that too helped to keep the scorching heat at bay. Nothing ever kept the dust out.

Gert looked up as Bridie entered, the screen door clicking shut behind her. 'All good?'

'Hard to say. Dad just lit out for parts unknown like his tail was on fire. And I don't know when he'll return. I don't understand. He seemed fine last night. Even after the engagement announcement.'

'About that…' Gert had been at the ball. 'Bit of a surprise.'

'Mm. More of a business arrangement than anything else.'

'Will we be seeing him here today?'

'Judah?' She had no idea when she'd be seeing him again. 'Er…not that I know of. Deals to cut, guests to farewell, that kind of thing.' She assumed…

'You should see if he wants to come over. I'm making ginger snaps.'

'I don't share your ginger snaps with just anyone.'

'Not even your fiancé?'

'Maybe if he asks nicely. Anyway, I'm heading for the darkroom. If anyone phones, come and get me.'

'You mean if your fiancé phones?'

'Or Reid.' Reid might want to talk with her about the way she was trying to shoehorn in on his tourism plans. 'Or Dad.' Just in case he saw fit to tell her what was wrong. 'But if anyone from the gallery calls, I'm not here. I'm out getting that final shot and it absolutely will be with them before opening night.'

Gert snorted and flapped her hand in Bridie's direction. 'Go.'

Bridie usually found developing film and pictures the old-fashioned way cathartic, but not today. Today her spacious darkroom reminded her of the lengths to which her father had gone to make it not remind her of the car boot she'd been bundled into during her abduction.

They'd fitted an old sitting room out with a revolving no-light no-lock door, and red LED strip lights. They'd covered windows and built benches and hung clothes lines for photos to hang from. These days her set-up was as good as any commercial dark-room in the city. Not that there were many of those left, given the advances in digital photography and automatic printing.

Thing was, she loved watching an image appear, ghostly at first, and then more certain, except today she wasn't feeling very certain about anything.

Why had her father left Devil's Kiss so suddenly? Had Judah's reappearance dredged up too many ugly memories for him? He'd never say that, of course. Keep going, move on, no need to obsess.

She and her father had each been given ten free psych sessions after the event, courtesy of some gov-ernment programme or other, and surely there was nothing left to talk about or even think about after that?

Facts were facts. Her father and Judah had been driving farm utes and between them had railroaded Laurence Levit and his zippy little sports car straight off the beaten track and into the superfine red dirt. Laurence's car, with her in the boot, had bumped over shrubbery and swerved hard before coming to a stop, bogged to the axels, and no amount of revving had done anything but dig them deeper.

Car doors had slammed. Bridie had started kicking and hadn't heard much, but she had heard the shot. Then Judah had been there, reaching for her, his face pale and shocked. A rufus red moon had hung low in the sky, silvery light glinting off the blade of the knife he'd used to cut the tape that had bound her hands and feet. She'd clung to him like a burr and his arms around her had been like bands of warm steel and he'd smelled like sweat and fear.

Her father hadn't tried to save Laurence at all, but Judah had tended the fallen man once he'd handed her off to her father. His efforts after the fact had earned him a charge of manslaughter rather than murder. He'd been just twenty, younger than she was now. Twenty and imprisoned on her account, and she'd always had a hard time finding the justice in that, but there was no point dwelling on it.

Move on, said her father, who'd been wholly uncomfortable in Judah's presence last night, and who'd taken off this morning for places unknown.

Bridie's big, beautifully appointed darkroom, which she usually took so much pleasure in, wasn't working for her today. Not when memories held sway. Better to be out and about, searching for that elusive final photograph for her exhibition—the one that would link all the rest of them. She already knew what needed to be in that shot. Fear. Foreboding. Freedom. Wonder.

All she had to do was look through the lens and find them.

'Change of plans, Gert. I'm heading out to take some shots and I'll be back before you leave.' Bridie sailed through the kitchen and ducked into the wet room for her boots and hat. 'Wish me luck.'

Two days later, with the weather radar promising late-afternoon thunderstorms if they were lucky, Judah finally paid her a visit. Gert was at Judah's now and her father still hadn't called, and if the sight of Judah strong and stern and unmistakably present made her unaccountably happy, probably best not to mention it.

'Greetings, fiancé of mine. How's it going?' she asked, aiming for breezy and doing a fair job of it if his almost smile was any indication.

'Not bad.'

She loved the rumble in his voice and the way he stood at the bottom of the steps, boots planted firmly in the dirt and his jeans clinging to strong legs. His cotton shirt had seen better days and the sleeves had been rolled up to expose corded forearms and prominent veins. He wore a black felt hat that dipped at the front, pinched at the top and sat level at the sides. He looked so quintessentially of the outback that it put her at ease. No matter where life had taken him, he'd grown up here, he knew this place the same way she did and there was comfort in that, and security.

'If only your wheeling, dealing billionaire buddies could see you now. What brings you by?'

'Gert said your father was away.'

'Yup.'

'For how long?'

'He didn't say.'

'I've been trying to get hold of him.' Judah studied her from beneath the brim of his hat and she wished she could see his eyes a little more clearly.

'Join the club. But if he's heading for Broome, he's likely well out of range.'

'What's in Broome?'

'My aunt.' The same aunt who'd travelled with Bridie to Paris all those years ago, both of them so totally out of their league they'd been easy pickings for a predator like Laurence. He'd been Bridie's modelling agent, and her aunt Bethany had never stood a chance against his calculated seduction. It had made his obsessive control over Bridie's career all the more insidious. His growing need to possess Bridie in every way possible had kicked in some time after that.

'How is Beth?'

'She blames herself for bringing Laurence into our lives and not realising how dangerous he was. She went into exile after the kidnapping. My father says she's too ashamed to show her face here.'

Judah frowned. 'That's cracked.'

'I know. I miss her hugs.' But he wasn't here to get the low-down on her dysfunctional family. 'Have you asked Reid about me joining you guys in the eco-tourism business?'

He nodded.

'And?'

'You're in.'

'Yes!'

'But it's growing as we put together a mission statement and growth goals.'

Say what now? 'Meaning?'

'I want to roll Reid's project into some broader, strategic land preservation plans I have for the area. Buy the Conrad place. See if your father will turn over some of Devil's Kiss land to the project.'

Mr Moneybags and clever along with it. How many times would she have to shift her take on this man, now that he was home? 'I'm about to head out and try and get some shots of the storm front coming in. Want to fill me in while I'm doing that?'

He looked towards the darkening sky. 'You want to be out in that?'

She so did. 'By my calculations it's going to break over the eastern channel plain. I aim to be just east of Pike's river crossing when it does.'

'And your father's not here to know if you'll return. I'll come.'

A blessing for protective neighbours. 'I'll drive.'

Five minutes later they were on their way, heading out in her Land Rover, and she tried not to obsess too much about how good Judah smelled. Some kind of body wash or soap with a hint of woody musk.

Expensive. Totally wasted on cattle, but definitely not wasted on her.

'Can I photograph you today?' And before he could say no or ask why: 'From a distance and for dramatic impact and perspective. You against the storm.' A fitting end to a set of photos that had always been about him, whether he knew it or not. 'A visual reminder for me that you're back where you belong and maybe now we can all move on.'

He looked out of the window and didn't answer, and she didn't push. He hadn't said no, and that meant he was thinking about it. If he at some point put himself in her camera's way she'd have her answer and they wouldn't need to talk about it ever again.

'Tell me about this exhibition of yours,' he said, and she had no problem at all with that request. 'Twenty of my best photos, printed and framed and about to be hung by professional curators in a light-filled gallery in fancy-pants Sydney. I need one more, and I'm fretting because I don't have it. The home run. The closer.'

'And this storm's going to give it to you?'

'Maybe.'

Already the sky was darkening to the west, the red dirt beginning to glow with that peculiar Armageddon light. Every contrast more vivid for not being bleached away by a relentless sun. Oncoming clouds, light at the edges and deepest grey in the middle, heavy with the promise of life-giving rain and the not-so-subtle threat of utter carnage.

Best not to get caught out in these fast-moving cloudbursts or they could be bogged for days, but she'd checked the wind direction earlier and figured they'd be able to stay just south of it.

Assuming the wind didn't change.

She headed off track and they cut across the loose dirt and scrub until she reached a shallow river crossing that the vehicle made short work of. She pulled up on a wave of dirt not long afterwards. From here the ground undulated to the north and west and flattened to the east and, with the right light and the right lens, subtle panorama contrasts could be found.

Set-up only took a few minutes. Tripod and cameras, lenses and light meter and Judah watching in silence, his very fine butt planted on the bonnet of her ride, knees bent and his boot heels hooked over the bottom rung of the bull bar.

'Storm's that way,' he rumbled when she snuck one too many glances in his direction.

'There's a food basket in the back if you're hungry.' She'd hit the fridge hard after he'd said he would join her. Double brie, quince paste and fancy crackers, she had 'em. Anzacs with wattle seed. Dark chocolate with raisins. Leftover ham sandwiches with real butter and Gert's magic relish. She had it all. A honeymoon basket, she'd thought with horror as she packed it, and had thrown in a couple of tins of baked beans and a round of salami in case they got stuck and also so that it wouldn't be a honeymoon basket any more. 'Drinks are in the esky.'

'Are you practising for when the lodges are built and you're bringing city photographers out here?'

'Yes. That's what I'm doing.'

Not trying to honeymoon him at all.

She'd made him grin and wasn't that a pretty sight? Her fingers itched for a camera even as she turned her back on him and bent to put her eye to the nearest camera and tripod. She wanted to play around with the zoom on this one. Heading back to her kit, she fished out a thin wire presser that would allow her to take a shot without pressing any buttons on the camera itself and creating movement she didn't want.

'You have a lot of gear.'

More than she needed, true. She'd once thought that taking the perfect shot was all about the gear, but experience had taught her differently. 'I don't need half of it. I have my favourite cameras and lenses and I know how to get the best out of them. Live and learn.'

She could feel him looking at her. The weight of his gaze skittered down her spine, but she refused to turn around. 'I kind of do better if I think of life as a learning curve. Mistakes are part of it.'

She took a few shots, fine-tuned the set-up, and then hauled the picnic basket onto the bonnet next to him, fished out a ham sandwich and waited for the storm. It might not pass this way. She might have misjudged it.

But she didn't think so.

Several minutes later Judah dug into the picnic basket too and she waited for some snide remark about her food choices.

Instead, he looked utterly lost for a split second before muttering, 'All right, I am here for this,' and digging in.

He ate as if he'd been underfed for years and she ate up that vulnerability in him because it made him less perfect in her eyes, more human.

And then the world turned amber and the storm clouds rolled in.

She got to work as he packed away the picnic, always aware of him but focused on capturing the landscape in front of her.

When he sauntered out in it, welcoming the rain that raced across the plain towards them, she photographed him. The strength in his silhouette and the acceptance of the storm as he stretched out his arms and received the opening lash of stinging rain. Violence. Renewal. Nothing was fixed, least of all him, but he was her focus. Judah Blake, killer and saviour, his hat in hand and his face tilted skywards. Vulnerable and mighty.

Back in this place that had built him.

It was a spur-of-the-moment thought that made her set her cameras to take continuous shots so she could join him, taking his hand and drawing him into a dance more elemental by far than the one they'd shared at the ball. They spun and they stomped and tears filled her eyes and she let them because they'd mingle with raindrops and wash away and who would know the difference?

'You're here,' she yelled, as lightning lit the sky and thunder rumbled and the rain pelted against them. 'I'm so glad you're here.'

And then he pulled her towards him, kissed her, and Bridie's careful, considered world exploded. When the debris cleared there was only rain and Judah, bringing her to life in ways she'd only ever dared to imagine.

Whatever he had to give, she could take it and it wasn't because of some nebulous sense of obligation for all that he had done. She wanted him.

He was back where he belonged, and she wanted him and that was all.

With a ruthlessness born of necessity, she drew him in.

CHAPTER FOUR

JUDAH HAD NEVER spun out of control so fast or slaked his need with such ruthlessness as he did now. Any gentleness he'd ever owned was gone, washed clear away as he framed her face with his hands, the better to devour her.

Bridie's hands were restless, trapped little fluttering sparrows at his chest, his waist, restless until she burrowed beneath his shirt and found skin.

He pulled her closer, his hardness impossible to conceal against her softness. His hands slid lower, lifting, positioning, unable to stop himself from thrusting against her.

Let me in.

She stilled. She tried to speak, or sigh, or maybe it was a protest, and that last thought was enough to douse him more thoroughly than any storm ever could. She didn't want this.

She didn't want him.

He wrenched his lips from hers and buried his face against her neck, nowhere near ready to let go of her and back away, but he had to.

'I'm sorry,' he grated.

'Hm?' She wove her fingers through his hair, keeping him there as she burrowed in closer.

He had no finesse. To rut against her much longer and that would be him gone, spent and sticky in his jeans—worse if he managed to get her out of her jeans because then there'd be nothing to halt his reckless, greedy descent into animal behaviour. Judah cursed and put his hands to Bridie's hips, put some air between them, the better to get his brain to start functioning.

Her gaze met his, glazed, confused. 'Why are we stopping? This is perfect. You're perfect.'

What a thing to say to a man like him. 'You don't even know me.'

She stepped back, eyes narrowing, and her hands went to her hips. 'I could get to know you. We could get to know each other and then maybe we could do more of the kissing.'

'It wouldn't stop at kissing.'

'So? I wouldn't want it to.'

'You don't know me.'

'But I'd like to.'

He tried again to make her see reason. To understand his position. 'You won't like what you find.'

'How do you know?'

'After what I did to you at the ball, how could you *not* know?'

She looked at him a good long while, mindless of the pelting rain, and then took a careful step back.

'You're too hard on yourself, Judah. But if you don't want what I'm offering, I can't make you take it. We can just call it a spur-of-the-moment kiss. Forget it ever happened.'

'Let's do that.' He'd spent too many years thinking of this woman as fragile and terrified and young. And maybe she'd grown in years but she had no experience with someone as greedy for touch as him. As unstable as him. Seven long years and counting, and he didn't trust himself to be the kind of lover she needed. 'Trust me, it's for the best.'

He tilted his face to the sky and let the stinging rain pellets wash him clean of his burning desire to get naked and dirty with a woman too pure for him to sully. 'Please. We're not doing this.'

Had she touched him again his resolve might have broken, but she turned away and trudged back to her cameras, and he could only hope those canvas covers she'd set up over the camera bodies had done enough to protect them from the downpour.

By the time he came back in and Bridie had packed up, the storm had passed and red mud caked his boots. She passed him a towel in silence, not quite meeting his gaze, and he gruffly thanked her.

He couldn't have felt any worse.

'Are you ready to leave?' she asked quietly.

Note to self: never reject a woman's advances without having your own ride home.

The drive back took three times as long on account of the rain, but they didn't get bogged and eventually they pulled up alongside his truck. Bridie's hair had started to dry in loose curls to frame her face. Such a perfect profile to go with her long lashes and flawless skin. No wonder the modelling world had gone all in for her. No wonder the predators had come circling.

He made a hasty exit and then turned back towards her—simultaneously glad to be out of the car and shamed by his mishandling of the afternoon. 'Look, Bridie, you're very beautiful.'

She had a fierce glare. 'Tell me something I don't know.'

'I haven't had sex in nearly eight years and my self-control is hanging by a thread. I don't want your gratitude, your pity or to hurt you, so it's best I stay away from you. See out this farce of an engagement and then leave you be. Do no harm. Savvy?'

'Got it. You're too big, bad and dangerous for innocent little me.' She stomped towards her homestead and he figured that was it, but then she turned and fixed him with a soggy kitten glare. 'Does anyone actually believe that's who you are?'

'You'd better believe it,' he yelled, because seriously. 'Shouldn't you be *thanking* me?'

'For being a tool? Why does that need praise?'

'For my restraint!'

For stopping when he did, so as not to overwhelm her? For *protecting* her? Again, because apparently it was his lot in life to get screwed over for love of protecting Miss Bridie Starr, bane of his existence.

I'm not depressed, he could tell Reid when he got back to the house.

I'm peeling out of my skin for want of a woman I dare not touch.

Apparently, I'm also an idiot.

Bridie spent the rest of the day seething, developing film, and coming to the bald realisation that she'd somehow just taken some of the best photos of her life. Danger. Foreboding. Homecoming. Pleasure.

The cameras she'd set up to take a shot every thirty seconds had caught those moments of them together and they were more beautiful than she could ever have imagined, and she couldn't ever show them to Judah, or anyone else, because he'd turned her down.

For reasons that made no sense.

'Complete and utter idiot,' she muttered the following morning as she dumped a tea bag into a huge mug and switched the jug on to boil some water. Because she'd had glorious love-soaked dreams all last night and she most certainly had not let the memory of yesterday's kisses go. *Hell, no.*

'Are you talking about my brother?' a voice wanted to know, from somewhere over near the doorway, and there stood Reid, hat in hand and hair unruly. 'Because he's also a surly bastard.'

'What are you doing here?'

'I came to talk business. I'm also here to check up on you and see if your father's home yet.'

And that was another reason for her foul mood. 'I haven't heard from him.'

'Have you spoken to your aunt?'

'Not since the trial,' she muttered darkly. 'And before you ask, I never cut her off. I love my aunt, even if she's *another* complete and utter moron. She blames herself for being taken in by a monster who courted her to get to me, and she's too ashamed to speak to me. I phoned. I wrote. I *begged* her to come see me. To forgive herself because I sure as hell didn't hold her responsible for someone else's insanity. Fat lot of good it did.'

'Er...right.'

'How come I didn't hear your helicopter?'

'I came on the dirt bike.'

She hadn't heard that either. Existing in a world of her own, her father would have said had he been around. Which he wasn't. *Stubborn old goat.* 'And you're also here on business, you said?'

'Yep. Tourist lodge business. What are your thoughts on retractable roofs and floor-to-ceiling glass windows?'

Bridie blinked.

'So that someone who, say, doesn't like feeling hemmed in and doesn't like sleeping indoors, doesn't have to sleep in a swag in the back of his ute every night.'

Reid sent her a beseeching look, inviting her to buy into his problems, but she didn't want to because she knew exactly where Reid's problems led. 'Judah?'

'Yep.'

Right.

'I just want to make it easier for him to get his life back, you know?' Reid continued. 'He's not always…coping. And it's the little stuff.'

Judah didn't exactly appear to be coping all that well with the big stuff either—if impromptu wanton kisses followed by a hasty retreat could be classified as such. Or maybe she was the only needy wanton person around here. 'What's not to love about disappearing ceilings and walls? Turn all the lights on and bring every insect for six kilometres around for a feed.'

'Okay, so my plans might need work,' Reid conceded. 'Wanna help?'

Two hours passed as they sketched cabin design after cabin design and talked about how best to accommodate eccentric guests with all sorts of needs. Reid's enthusiasm was contagious, and Bridie's interest in putting lodges on the ridges became real. She *wanted* this project to succeed. Two hours and three arguments later, they had a cabin layout they both liked. Bridie sat back, pleased with their progress. 'I'm on board with this.'

'Don't sound so shocked.'

'But I *am* shocked. I want these eco-tourism plans to work. I want to bring people here.'

Reid grinned and punched a fist in the air. 'I knew

it! And you're going to be a world-famous photographer soon. That's a given.'

She put her palms to her face and rubbed as butterflies found a home in her stomach at the thought of the final picture she'd chosen for the exhibition. 'I'm going to try.' The words came out muffled. 'What if the media fixates on my past, instead of my work? Drags me through the mud, and Judah too? And by extension, you.' She lowered her hands. Her fears came from a place of experience. 'You were probably too young to remember the way the press treated the story.'

'I was at boarding school. Believe me, I remember.'

Oh. 'Sorry.'

'Not your fault, but you're right when it comes to not wanting to stir up that hornet's nest.' Reid picked up a pencil and began to number the cabin plans. 'I want to protect my big mean-dog brother. He's not nearly as tough and indestructible as he thinks he is. I thought your father would be here to help me.'

But her father wasn't here. 'How can I help?'

'Judah wants to talk about putting some Jeddah Creek, Conrad's and Devil's Kiss land into a conservation trust. Get your father to give him a call so he can get moving on that.'

'What else? And by that I mean something that's vaguely within my control.'

'Maybe invite him around for breakfast or call him once a day or something, so he knows you're okay over here. Same way you and Tom used to tag-team me after Dad died. Just…check in once a day. He worries about you over here on your own, and so do I.'

'I'll group-text you both a photo every day.' Problem solved.

'He could use a friend.'

'Reid—' She shook her head, hoping he'd understand without her having to explain. 'My feelings for your brother are complicated. Friendship's a stretch. There's so much in the way of it.'

Physical attraction. Saviour status. Rejection…

'What if you try befriending him in Sydney? Do stuff together. Sightsee and all that. That could work.' Reid sounded so hopeful. 'But don't be surprised if he stays out all night. He does that. I think it's because he can't stand sleeping inside four walls.'

Maybe she could order a roll-out bed to put on a balcony. Or she could just walk with him through the city all night long, befriending him. Which would make her the grumpiest emerging landscape photographer ever. 'I will be a sphinx in the face of your brother's strange sleeping habits. No comment.'

'Thanks.'

She enjoyed watching Reid striding past his teen years and turning into a truly caring and responsible young man. 'That's if he decides to come to Sydney with me at all. He might not.'

'He said he would, didn't he? My brother keeps his word.'

'Yes, but maybe I shouldn't have pressed him to

come with me in the first place.' She'd been thinking of her own challenges when it came to stepping
out of her comfort zone. 'It honestly never occurred
to me that Judah might have issues with those surroundings, and frankly it should have.' She needed
to stop clinging to her Judah-as-Superman fantasy.
It was self-indulgent at best and had the potential to
be downright destructive.

'I'll go alone.' Gulp. 'That's fine. I'll give your
brother a call and let him know I've had a change of
plans. I can invent a girlfriend who's joining me or
something. Give the man an out.'

'I didn't say to sideline him,' objected Reid. 'A
change of scenery might do him good. What's wrong
with sticking to the current plan and being there for
him, if he needs a friend?'

'Yeah, but…' Reid didn't know about the kissing.

'Don't make me pull the *You owe him compassion and understanding* card.' Reid looked utterly
serious. 'Because I will.'

'Oh, that's harsh.'

Reid glared.

'Can we agree that I need to at least give him the
option of not going with me to Sydney seeing as, by
your own admission, he's not coping with the little
things?'

Reluctantly, Reid agreed.

Bridie did phone Judah later that afternoon. Not
much of a phone conversationalist, Judah, and Bridie was little better.

They did 'hey' and 'hope this isn't a bad time to call' before she got down to the business of giving him an out when it came to him joining her in Sydney. 'Hey, so I'm thinking of heading to Sydney a day earlier than planned, and that's probably not going to work for you, so maybe you might want to rethink joining me at all?'

'Is this about the kissing?'

'Ah, no? Not entirely. As in, I'm aware there'll be no kissing if you do come.'

'It's for your own good.'

Did he seriously believe what he was saying? She had a feeling he did. How did such a good man develop a mindset that he was no good at all? Had his years in prison damaged him beyond repair? 'Yes, well. Not sure I agree with you there, but moving on. You don't have to come.'

'Is your father meeting you there?'

'Er…' She still hadn't heard from him. 'I'm going to go with no.'

'He still hasn't been in touch,' he guessed flatly.

'No, and I'm worried about him, but that's a different conversation.'

'I can come to Sydney a day earlier with you. Not a problem.'

Oh. 'Even if it's awkward between us?'

'When is it not?'

The man had a point. 'Okay, well, thank you. Wednesday departure, then, and a Saturday return.' How had she managed to add another day to the trip rather than cutting him loose? *Good job, dimwit. Really good job.* 'It's really not a problem if I go alone. You saw me at the ball, navigating people with ease.' Slight stretch of the truth there. 'I am all prepped.'

'Good to hear, but I'm still coming with you.' She could hear the iron in his voice. 'I gave you my word.'

CHAPTER FIVE

SYDNEY HARBOUR GLITTERED like the jewel it was as the plane banked hard, allowing Bridie a bird's eye view of the bridge, the Opera House, the skyscrapers and the roofscapes of the suburbs beyond. She and Judah had flown first-class commercial from Cairns, picking up the final leg of an inbound plane's international flight, and from the moment she'd boarded, Bridie had been having a champagne experience.

And her pleasure might just be contagious, given Judah's wry grin every time food or beverages were offered.

She'd opted for an easy-travel fabric—synthetic, lightweight, no crush—and the draping neckline of her shirt likely plunged a little too low, and her shoes were once again sky-high, but she'd added a scarf in every imaginable shade of blue and draped it just so, and she was surviving the nakedly admiring glances strangers kept giving her with surprising nonchalance.

Pretty woman. She'd owned that label once and made a career of it. It had brought Laurence into her life, but it had also opened her up to the world beyond Devil's Kiss, and that world had once been her oyster. Maybe it could be again.

All she needed was confidence enough to seize it. Blazing confidence.

Except for those moments when she kept fiddling with the bracelet Judah had given her, or twisting her engagement ring around and rubbing at the stones with the pad of her thumb and hoping to hell those pretty stones didn't fall out on her watch. Maybe if she sat on her hands...that might help, but then Judah would probably ask if she was scared of flying and she would have to either nod and lie or confess to their 'engagement' bothering her more than she wanted to admit.

He was all easy control, with a coiled energy simmering beneath that mighty fine skin, and if she could just duplicate that combination, borrow some of his armour for the weekend, that would be great. Shake off the nervous tension that not even two glasses of very fine champagne could dim.

There would be a car and a driver waiting to take them to the hotel once they landed. She'd brought two pictures with her for delivery to the gallery, all bubble-wrapped and boxed, so as to stay undamaged during the trip. The curator had seen the images already and immediately wanted to hang both—a move Bridie had yet to give the go-ahead. Judah hadn't seen them, and if she wanted to use them in the exhibition, he needed to.

Not that he was truly recognisable. More of an outline bitten by rain, but it was him.

There was such a thing as permission, and she didn't have it and that was a problem.

Just ask him.

'Judah?'

He looked up from the newspaper he'd been reading, eyes like flint.

She chickened out at the last moment. 'Would you like to swap seats? The view's really good.'

'Keep looking,' he murmured. 'You're the landscape photographer.'

And there was her cue. 'Sometimes I take pictures of people. People in landscapes. Sometimes they turn out really good. Good enough to exhibit.'

He knew exactly what she was talking about, she'd stake her life on it. But he made no comment at all as he turned his attention back to the newspaper.

'If art is a journey, then you're part of my journey and your freedom is the finish line when it comes to my current body of work,' she continued doggedly.

'Do what you want with the photos you took,' he muttered, without looking up.

'I'd like you to see the one I have in mind for the exhibition,' she pressed. 'You're in it. You're facing away from the camera, but it's you.'

'If you think it's good enough for the exhibition then it is. I don't need to see it.'

'Do I have your permission to show it?'

He nodded curtly.

'Can I get that in writing? Not that I don't trust you to keep your word, but the gallery needs the surety.'

'I'll sign their form.'

'Thank you. Would you like to see the photo?' She had it on her phone. 'There's another one too, but I'm not as sure about that one. I'd really like you to look.'

'I'll see it on the night, won't I?'

'Yes, but…' He looked up, pinning her with his gaze. 'Okay, right. It'll be a happy surprise.'

Stop fussing, Bridie. He's said yes. What more do you want?

Apart from everything he was willing to give.

The hotel was everything a majestically placed five-star branded establishment should be, with the manager, a majestic example of understated yet reverential welcome, greeting them himself. 'Mr Blake, of course. And Miss Starr. You'll be occupying the Bridge Suite.'

This was news to Bridie, and she glanced at Judah for confirmation.

'It's bigger,' he said.

'Yes, indeed,' said the manager. 'Four hundred square metres of premium living space, with two bedrooms, living and dining areas, spa, stunning harbour views from floor-to-ceiling windows, a substantial terrace area and twenty-four-hour concierge.'

'Looking forward to it,' she said faintly. Guess being a gazillionaire opened up all sorts of doors, walls, windows and so on.

'Is there somewhere your artwork needs to go?' the fellow asked, and yes, yes, there was.

'I'm expecting someone from the Bridge West Gallery to collect it this afternoon.'

'But of course, Miss Starr. And will you be keeping it with you until then?'

'Thank you, yes.'

'I shall inform you when they arrive. We have the work of some of their artists here in the hotel, although the Bridge Suite, from memory, currently houses a small Olsen and a Noonan.'

She knew one of those names. 'Lovely.'

'They are of course available for purchase.'

'Of course.'

A porter materialised beside them. 'Andrew, please see Mr Blake, Miss Starr and their belongings to the Bridge Suite,' the manager said.

Andrew nodded and a few minutes later saw them settled into the most luxurious apartment Bridie had ever been in. 'How much is all this costing?'

'No idea,' said Judah from the terrace area. 'But it's on me.'

'But I said *I'd* pay. I was the one who invited you here.'

He shrugged, smiled, and suddenly looked inexplicably amused. 'What's a Noonan?'

'No idea.' But suddenly the amazing view of one of the most famous harbours in the world glittered that little bit brighter. There was so much movement out on the water, what with all the ferries and the boats motoring along and a deep rolling swell beneath them. So many people over near the Opera House, walking, eating at the restaurants that dotted the quay. That stunning view, and the utter indulgence of the spa room and the rest of the suite, almost drew her attention away from Judah, who'd ditched his business blazer and tie but kept the immaculate white shirt beneath. He was busy rolling up his sleeves, and, sure, the harbour view was amazing but nothing could compete with corded forearms, broad palms and long, strong fingers at work.

Maybe his bare chest could compete.

The muscles of his back.

What if he had a bath and then stood up to sluice down, facing the window? She could be watching from the doorway. Voyeurism had never been so appealing.

'Something wrong with my arms?'

Was that a rumble in his voice or a purr?

'Not that I can see.' Nope, all good. She refused to be embarrassed because she'd been caught ogling him. Time to check out the other view. White sails, blue skies, the play of light reflecting off skyscraper walls and windows. So busy. Was she ready for all that?

There was no rush, was there? She had time to catch the breath Judah had stolen.

They settled in while a maid unpacked their clothes into separate wardrobes in different rooms. The person from the gallery came to collect her work, and left her with the promise that the collection would be hanging in the gallery from midday tomorrow, and if she wanted to drop by earlier and introduce herself to the staff she was most welcome to. Mr Blake was also most welcome, and had needed no introduction. The gallery guy knew who he was and stood ready to fawn all over him at the slightest encouragement.

Judah didn't give it.

She had the unsettling feeling he was almost as uncomfortable with their fancy hotel suite as she was.

'Okay, famous person,' she said when they left. 'I'm for walking across the bridge and past Luna Park and ending up at Wendy Whiteley's secret garden. It's been years since I was a proper shut-in. I'm willing to find out just how far I've come. Want to join me?'

She turned from that beautiful view to find him watching her through narrowed eyes.

'Okay, make that please come with me. Yes, I'd be using you as a crutch. You're spectacular in that role, by the way. I've never felt so safe. But if you walk with me today, what's to say that tomorrow I won't walk to the gallery on my own? And back? With a detour through the shopping area at The Rocks. I could stop for a snack all by myself in the most crowded coffee shop I can find.'

'You could do that today,' he said drily.

'I could.' She tried to inject a little surety into

that statement. 'I might need to work my way up to "I will", hence my invitation. I'm crowd-challenged, not stupid.'

He smiled as if he couldn't help it, and it was a wondrous thing, watching this man relax into his skin.

'I guess I could be of use,' he said, and there was that purr again. Did he know he could send goose-bumps dancing beneath her skin at the sound of it? Or that he was making her want to offer herself up to him all over again and to hell with being a virgin? She could go out and get rid of that here in the city and be right back in time to accommodate him. In her dreams this was entirely possible.

In reality, she'd never do such a thing, so if anything was going to change in order for them to get together it would have to be him. Not that she was trying to pressure him, because she wasn't. Kisses were out, friendship was in. Their fake engagement was nothing more than her being willing to wear a pretty ring.

They walked the bridge. They found Wendy's garden with its towering fig trees and magical view of the bridge. They caught a water taxi back and it took them beneath the bridge and deposited them at Circular Quay just as dusk turned the light that particular shade of purple. She itched for her camera, but she'd made a conscious decision not to bring it with her, the better to simply observe.

Not once had she felt threatened by her surroundings or other people.

Judah too seemed to take the city in his stride. He didn't have a lot to say, or maybe his body language spoke for him. Walking relaxed him, or being out in the open did. He hadn't like being cooped up, no matter how enormous the hotel suite. The restaurant they ended up at had an outdoor eating and bar area with a mighty harbour view. One drink turned into two as he asked her what a successful exhibition could do for her. What else she wanted to photograph. Where else in the world she wanted to go.

'Baby steps,' she replied. 'I'm all about getting this exhibition squared away, never mind what might come next.'

'Think big,' he urged. 'Go hard. Figure out your next steps now, before you need to take them.'

'Yet there I was offering myself to you in the rain and you were all no, no, I'm far too much for you to handle. You thought I should start small.'

His fingers stilled on the glassware in front of him. His gaze met hers, fierce fire banked by shadows.

'You give contradictory advice,' she continued. 'Just saying.'

No argument followed, just silence, tense and heavy.

'But I'm not dwelling on that. Much. Maybe a little bit. But I am willing to move on. Maybe we should give friendship a go.' Subtlety be damned.

'We could start by telling each other something only a friend would know.'

'Never eat from my plate,' he offered.

'Former model here. I barely eat from my plate, let alone someone else's. Thank you for sharing, though. Not your food, obviously, but your thoughts on sharing food.' Befriending a billionaire ex-con who had rejected you was hard. 'We're sharing a bottle of wine, though. Hurrah.'

'Now you,' he murmured. 'Spill.'

What was something about her only a friend would know? She barely had any friends beyond Gert. 'I have a night light in my bedroom. It's cunningly disguised as a power socket plug-in that shows where the door is, but it's a night light. I can't sleep without one.'

He didn't make fun of her. She gave him points for that.

'If I'm in a room I like to face the door,' he offered.

'What if there's more than one door? Like here?' The balcony eating area had several ways in and out.

'Then it's my back to the wall.'

Good thing they'd been able to accommodate him. 'None of the vehicles we own have boots. It's tray tops, twin cabs or Land Rovers. I'm very indulged.'

'That's all we have. They're practical.'

Something in common at last! 'Does this mean we're best buds now?'

'No.'

'But worth a try, right?' Was his sense of humour

really that dry? Did he even have a sense of humour? Who would know?

He caught the eye of a hovering waiter and nodded for the bill before returning his attention to her. It settled on her like a weight she wanted to carry with her always. 'Definitely worth a try.' He waited a beat. 'I was angry with you when I heard you were a shut-in for a lot of years. I wanted you to soar so that my sacrifice was worth something.'

She didn't know what to say.

'I understand trauma a lot better now. Taking your time. Finding your way. Figuring out how to fit in. That's where I am right now. Inside.'

'I know.'

'That's why it's not a good idea for you to get too invested in me. I'll only let you down.'

'I know that's what you think.' She'd been there. She'd spent years in that place he was now. And she wept for him.

The bill came and they were out of there a couple of minutes later. The walk back to the hotel was downright romantic, given the artistry of the city lights and the lingering warmth of the day.

Silence helped.

The way they fell into step, shoulder to shoulder.

He didn't talk. Not even when they reached the hotel and the lift doors opened and she stepped inside and he didn't.

'You're staying out for a while?' May as well make it easy for him.

'Yes.'

He didn't even try to come up with an excuse for not wanting to return to the rooms. This beautiful, broken man who refused to admit he was having a hard time fitting back into a world without bars. His dignity, pride, or even just his strongly developed sense of survival, wouldn't allow him to show weakness at all. And Bridie, forewarned, projected sphinx-like serenity. 'See you in the morning. I'm aiming for breakfast at eight in the suite. I'll save you a seat.'

'You do that.'

Not exactly a commitment to join her, was it? The lift doors began to close.

He stayed facing her even as he took a step back. 'Sleep well, Bridie. Give Noonan my regards.'

And then there was nothing but her reflection in mirrored metal doors.

CHAPTER SIX

IT WAS AFTER one in the morning, and Judah was heavy eyed and dreaming of sleep as the Manly ferry docked at Circular Quay and someone on the intercom told him and the cuddling young couple at the back of the ferry, and the old woman sitting inside the well-lit interior, to please alight and have a good night and that the next service would leave at five-thirty a.m.

Shame about the service stopping for the night, because he'd have ridden that ferry until dawn if he could have, and if that made him odd then so be it. Being out on the harbour soothed him. He'd missed the movement that came of travelling somewhere. That and horizons—he'd missed them too. After growing up in the outback, not being able to see a horizon every time he looked up or looked out had nearly broken him.

But he'd done it. Made it out, still young and fit and wealthy enough to live a life of riches and privilege others could only dream of. Viscount Blake, with a brother who worried about him and a beautiful woman who wanted his kisses, and, failing that, wanted to be his friend.

All told, he was a very lucky man.

He let the fifty-dollar note in his pocket drift to the floor as he passed the old woman on his way to the exit ramp. She had a trolley with her—one of those two-wheeled contraptions with a handle and a little seat—and a backpack as well. For reasons he couldn't quite pinpoint he figured she had nowhere to go. Ride the ferry, kill some time. Try not to give in to quiet desperation.

'Young man?'

He paused.

'You dropped your money.'

She had a look of steadfast honesty about her. As if it was all she had left and she wasn't giving it up without a fight. It was the same way he felt about his integrity. Other people could think what they liked about him, but *he* knew he was a man of principle.

'No, I didn't.' He picked it up and handed it to her, and helped her with her trolley as she tottered down the ferry ramp ahead of him.

'You're not from around here, are you?' she asked.

'No. And you? Where are you from?'

'Long story.' She had kind eyes and a twin suit with pearl buttons, this elderly woman with no home.

'Buy you a coffee over there if you have the time.' He nodded towards an all-night coffee house. 'I have time.'

By the time they parted, Mary—her name was

Mary—had a room in a nearby hotel for a week, breakfast included, all the money he had on him, and his phone number. She'd worked as her late husband's bookkeeper all her life. Her husband had been a gambler, but she'd always had a roof over her head. Until he died and the creditors came calling.

'My accountant is looking for a bookkeeper,' he told her. 'You'd have to relocate to a small town in western Queensland and you might not like either the place or the work, but I can vouch for the people. If you're ever interested in taking a look, give me a call. I'll get you a plane ticket there and back so you can have an interview.'

'Sweet man, don't waste your money. I'm sixty-seven years old. Who's going to employ me?'

'Well, the accountant's seventy, so you still have a few years on him.'

She laughed and it was a hearty sound. He liked that. Other people's indifference to her plight hadn't yet broken her. 'I'll give it some thought. Thing is, I've lived in this city all my life. I don't know if I can change.'

'I understand.'

'You're a good man.'

'I want to be.'

By the time he reached his hotel on the harbour it was three a.m. and his hyper watchfulness had dimmed to a casual interest in his surroundings, made all the more possible by the lack of people.

He nodded to the night staff. Clocked their features and the names on their badges and headed for the suite. His room had a wall full of windows and a sliding door out onto the terrace, and maybe this was the moment he'd finally bed down inside a building rather than out.

The bed on offer looked softer than a cloud, all fluffy whites and soft greys with some navy stripes thrown in for variety. There was a feather and down quilt. Or maybe an even flasher just down model. Definitely no shortage of pillows. This was bedmaking at its finest, complete with turn-down service, slippers and a chocolate on his pillow, which he ate because it was there.

If this much bed wooing didn't fix him, nothing would.

He thought of homeless bookkeeper Mary and her fear of the unknown.

He thought about Bridie the shut-in and how far she'd come.

And shucked down to his boxer briefs and gave the bed a try.

Bridie woke early enough to catch the sunrise and this time she reached for her camera. She loved this time of day when the light still glowed softly and magic stirred the land. Judah lay sleeping on a recliner on the terrace. She didn't mean to wake him— she thought she was being stealthy and quiet—but when she turned back after getting her shots his eyes were open, even if shadowed by the forearm he'd flung across his face.

'I couldn't help myself. Look at that view.'

'What time is it?'

'Quarter to six.' Give or take.

He didn't groan, but it was close. A proper fiancée might have asked him what time he got in. A proper fiancée might have stayed out all night with him, but she was neither of those, although she did know full well that it had been after three before he got in. 'I ordered coffee from room service. Shall I order one for you? How do you take it?'

'However it comes.' Suddenly he was on his feet and stretching, and it was impossible not to look. He wore only boxers and there was not an inch of the man's body that hadn't been sculpted and honed to perfection.

'Let's try that again,' he rasped. 'Strong and black, no sugar and cream on the side.'

'I'm on it.' She left him on the terrace and called his order in, and if she snapped a couple of stealth photos of him out there enjoying the view for her own private collection, well, she would wrestle with her conscience later.

She so rarely got to photograph people—that part was true.

The novelty of it was making her take stealth photos of this man—a rationalisation so blatantly false she rolled her eyes and vowed to stop lying to herself.

He was beautiful.

Beautiful and dangerous and so utterly compelling that whenever she saw him she itched to capture a little piece of him to keep. A glance. The cut of his jaw. His stance. She wanted to memorise them.

Oh, hell. That was stalking behaviour.

Nausea crawled down her throat and threatened to return with bile. She found the shots and deleted them, conscience cleared, but the bitter aftertaste of obsessive behaviour still lingered. No one deserved to be the unwilling focus of someone else's obsession. She knew that better than anyone.

So when the coffees came and Judah entered the kitchen to get his, she studied him with a detached eye for detail and a determination to treat him with respect. 'I took a look at the clothes I packed last night—bear with me because I am going somewhere with this story...'

Maybe he hid a smile behind the rim of his coffee cup, and maybe he didn't, but somehow she could sense him unwinding into the space she'd left for him.

'And I'm heading out this morning to find new clothes to wear tonight. And because I wish to be friends with you, I'm not asking you to come with me and endure hours of boredom. You do you, I'll do me, and I'll be back after I've been to the gallery. I'm aiming for a late lunch up here in the suite, because I'll have had enough of people by then and I'll need to recharge before the exhibition opening.'

'Sounds like a plan.'

'I really would like for you to be there for me this evening,' she continued doggedly. 'I'm going to be nervous.' She was *already* nervous. 'But you don't need to be there if it's really not your thing.'

'In the eyes of the world you're my fiancée. It's your first show. I'll be there.'

'If I take your hand and squeeze, it'll mean I need to get out of there before I have a meltdown. And I know artists are known for being temperamental, fragile, or all ego, but I'd rather not be seen as any of those things.'

'Even if you are?'

She sipped her coffee and took strength from it. 'Yes, even if I am those things underneath. I don't want to show that vulnerability to the world. I think that's something you might understand and I'm asking for your help.'

'You'll get it.'

'Thank you.' She could ask for nothing more. 'Coffee's good.'

'Very.'

'I took pictures of you this morning when you were out on the terrace.'

'I know.'

'I deleted them.'

He said nothing.

'You dazzle me. You have such presence. All that coiled strength and power. I want to see how it works, break it down into understandable pieces, but I'm not a stalker and the thought that I'm beginning to act like one horrifies me. I won't ever take pictures of you again without asking your permission. I think that's important for both of us to understand. You have my word.'

'Okay.'

She could see his chest rise and fall beneath the thin cotton of the T-shirt he'd thrown on, along with sweatpants. 'You do realise I'm sharing a full basket of vulnerabilities with you here?'

'They weren't exactly hidden.'

Ouch, Judah. Ouch. 'You could reciprocate by revealing one of your many flaws. You might be scared of emus.' She loved it when he smiled, no matter how small. 'No?'

'No.'

'Razorbacks?' Those huge wild pigs were mean mothers.

'No.'

'Ghosts?'

'I'll give those their due,' he offered. 'I have a few.'

But he didn't name them and she didn't press. Why on earth had she mentioned ghosts to a man who had killed to protect her? And then lost both his parents less than a year ago, while in prison for his sin? 'They can dance with mine,' she muttered. 'They might even be the same ghosts. I bet you're afraid of mice.'

'In plague proportions? You betcha.'

See? They could have a meaningful, getting-to-know-you conversation if they tried. It took great patience and good coffee. And now she needed to retreat and leave him be, because she wasn't pushy or needy or utterly infatuated with him. She was Bridie Starr of Devil's Kiss station and life was full of joy and pain and growth and heartache and that was all just part of living. And dammit she wanted to live. 'So, I'll see you this evening?'

He nodded.

She turned away.

'Hey.' He'd waited until she was almost to her room. 'For what it's worth, you dazzle me too.'

By six o'clock that evening, Bridie's bravado seemed to have fled. Judah watched with growing concern as she refused a bite to eat and started pacing instead, pausing every now and then to look at the paintings on the wall and in doing so somehow make her silhouette look even smaller.

'How many people need to be at this opening for it to be a success?' he asked, and she wrapped her arms around her middle and looked blankly towards him.

He tried again. 'How many pictures do you need to sell for the exhibition to be a success?'

'I'm sure the gallery has a percentage in mind, but I don't know it. Sell-out show sounds good, though.'

He could help with her sell-out-show wish. He'd already secured one picture by calling through to the gallery this afternoon. He'd agreed that whatever picture of him she'd chosen to display could be part of her exhibition but hell if he was going to let it end up on someone else's wall. The gallery director had initially told him it wasn't for sale. Money had taken care of that objection. She'd promised not to sell the picture to anyone but him.

'Does this outfit look arty enough?'

She looked to him for an answer, but how would he know what arty looked like? Didn't arty people slink around in black trousers and turtlenecks? Or was that look owned by successful tech titans these days?

Bridie wore a vivid blue silk top streaked with grey and the burnt orangey brown of the channel country she called home. Sleeves to her elbows, the neckline as high and tight as one of his shirts. The top angled in towards her impossibly tiny waist and with it she wore severe grey trousers that flared at the bottom and didn't go anywhere near to covering lace-up black boots. It was a fashion look, as far as he could tell, and she wore it very well. 'Yes. You look fantastic.'

'Fantastically arty though?'

'Yes.' And he looked like a suit, because he only had a few looks and one of them was outback scruffy and another was prison rough and neither would do here. 'How did you get into modelling in the first place? Was it something you wanted?'

'Oh.' She looked momentarily surprised by his question. 'No. I didn't think about my looks at all much when I was growing up. I was just me and there was no one around much to see me anyway.'

'So how did you start?'

'I was in Melbourne with Aunt Beth for my fifteenth birthday and we'd gone to David Jones department store because she was going to buy me some make-up. That was her gift to me. It was the first time I'd ever seen those little make-up booths with women just standing around looking beautiful and waiting to make other people look beautiful too.' She smiled at the memory. 'Everything was so *glossy*. So there we were and this make-up lady had just given me smoky eyes and cheekbones and then this beautifully dressed power woman rushed past and then backed right up and pointed at me and said, "*You*, come with me." It was fashion week. An hour later I was walking down the catwalk, filling in for a model who hadn't turned up. And that was that. Hello, modelling career, with my aunt as my manager.'

'Did you like it?'

'I loved the clothes, the make-up artists and hair stylists fussing over me, and the way I could sometimes barely recognise myself after they were done. Yeah. And then they took me off the catwalk and turned the camera on me and I got to see what great photographers could do with light and colour and settings and perspective and I was hooked. I wanted *that*, photography, only by that time Laurence was my manager and my aunt's lover and he didn't want that for me at all. He got more controlling. Started coming to every shoot. It only got creepier from there. I think he wanted a dress-up doll.'

Even after sitting at trial and hearing that Bridie had been beaten and kidnapped but not sexually abused, he hated thinking about what might have happened had Laurence not been stopped.

'Anyway. It cured me of wanting to be anyone's fantasy image ever again.' She crossed her arms in front of her and cupped her elbows.

He tilted his head, digesting her words. 'So how are you going to manage your public image and keep the crazies away this time around?'

'I'm kind of hoping that being engaged to Australia's most dangerous ex-con billionaire is going to do the trick. And I know it's wrong of me to put you in the position of having to protect me again but...' She looked away. 'You're the best there is.'

That right there was the reason there could never be anything between them. Her expectations were totally at odds with the screwed-up, shut-down mess of a man he was beneath all that protective saviour gloss she kept painting on him.

'Would you like a drink?' she asked next and gestured towards the mini bar. 'Something to help settle my nerves. Not champagne, that'd go straight to my head.'

'There's beer.'

'Perfect.'

'Okay.'

He fetched one for each of them and put music on. He watched her take the tiniest sip, not nearly enough to settle her nerves so he held out his hand

and said, 'Dance with me,' because holding her in his arms and not putting any moves on her was clearly his torture method of choice and he figured it would keep her mind off the exhibition for a while.

His dancing hadn't improved since the ball and neither had hers, but they made do, in the shadow of one of the most famous bridges in the world and with a light show spinning across the Opera House sails.

'People are going to love your art,' he told her. 'You're going to charm them with your arty-looking self and talent until they beg for more.'

A dimple dotted her cheek when she smiled. 'I'll hold that thought close.'

'No problem. Seriously. Your photos are amazing. You've got this.'

They made it to the gallery with ten minutes to spare. The owner, Sara, greeted them with a relieved smile, plied them with alcohol and introduced them to the rest of the gallery staff. The gallery floor was grey concrete and the walls a severe kind of white that only gallery spaces could pull off. It pushed people's attention towards the art, he supposed, as, drink in hand, he turned his attention towards the photographs on the walls.

He recognised some of them because they were ones Bridie had sent him over the years, only the ones she'd sent him had been schoolbook size. These ones were larger, some of them much larger. The two panoramas on display, one below the other, ran the length of the wall.

Sara drew Bridie away, talking business Judah didn't need to know, so he planted himself in front of a red river gum tree he knew of old and studied the people who came through the door. Bridie would find him when she wanted to, and meanwhile the room began to fill. A wealthy couple to start with, a tourist, a student with a date he wanted to impress and maybe they were only there for the free food and drinks, but not all of them had free food in mind.

When one of the gallery staff discreetly enquired whether he was interested in purchasing the red river gum, because another guest was interested in buying it, he said no, and moved to plant himself in front of the next picture.

Bridie played the shy emerging artist to perfection as gallery owner, Sara, introduced her to various guests. Judah left them to it, watching from a distance and trying not to look too menacing. He'd just turned to study the pair of panoramas again when someone backed into him.

He turned. She turned, and flushed beet red to match her hair. Not a threat—though he checked his pockets to make sure that his wallet was still there. It was.

'I'm so sorry,' she began. 'I need a rear-vision mirror—oh!' Her eyes widened as her gaze reached his face. 'It's you.'

'Do I know you?' He didn't recognise her.

'No?' Now was the time for her to introduce herself, but she didn't. 'I mean, no, you don't know me and I don't know you, but you're the one in the picture.' She gestured towards a wide doorway leading towards another part of the gallery. 'In there.'

Judah raised his eyebrows. 'Ah.'

'It's very compelling.'

'Is it, now?' If he could get away without looking at it this evening, he would. Put simply, he didn't want to have to look at his mug in a photo and pretend he thought of it as art.

'My friends were joking that you couldn't possibly be real, but here you are.'

'Here I am.' *Save me. Save me now.*

'Such a shame it's already sold.'

To him, yes. It had better be. He looked for more red dots below the paintings in the room. Three sales out of nine paintings in the first half-hour. Clearly it was time to add more purchasing weight to the show. 'If you'll excuse me.'

He caught the eye of a gallery assistant who was at his side in an instant.

'May I help you, sir?'

'I want to buy the two panoramas over there.'

'Certainly.' Moments later, they too had red dots underneath them.

'How do I pay?'

'Ms Starr's instructions are that you don't pay. Whatever you want from the collection is yours.'

That wouldn't do at all. 'Do you know who I am?'

'Of course, Mr Blake, sir.' The man was unflappable. Judah swung between being righteously annoyed and reluctantly impressed by the man's intransigence. 'Whatever pieces you want here tonight are yours. Ms Starr's orders and already cleared with management.'

How generous. He didn't want any part of it. 'In that case, I believe you misunderstood my intentions. I'm buying the panoramas on behalf of Sirius Corp, not in a personal capacity, therefore Ms Starr's offer cannot apply.' Sirius Corp was the name of the company he'd formed with Reid and Bridie to build the eco retreats. 'If there's a third panorama on offer, I want that too.'

The man beamed with bright enthusiasm. 'There is one other, and of course your purchase on behalf of another entity is a different matter altogether. If you'll excuse me, I'll see to the paperwork.'

Money. His family had always had it. Never before had he wielded it with such cynical understanding that success could be bought. Or at the very least, the impression of success could be bought.

He helped himself to a canapé—some kind of smoked salmon, cheese and chives in pastry option—and headed towards the wide doorway that would lead him deeper into the gallery.

He didn't see the photo at first. Not until he walked past the floating wall in the middle of the next room, but there was no avoiding it after that.

The picture took up at least half of the wall and he could all but feel the storm bearing down on him. True to her word, you couldn't see his face, but every

line in his body screamed with a primal summons
for nature to have a go at him: bring it on and don't
make the mistake of thinking that taking him down
was ever going to be easy.

Was this how he looked whenever a prison fight
had been in the offing?

'Powerful, isn't it?' said a voice from beside him,
and it was the gallery owner, whose name he now
couldn't recall. 'But then, you're a very powerful
man these days.'

'Is she going to let me have it?'

'Buy it? No. As I mentioned on the phone, it's not
for sale. But it's yours for the taking, nonetheless. No
one else gets to have it. Have you seen the other one?'

'What other one?'

'Turn around.'

He turned and this time he felt the impact of the
picture like a punch to the gut.

All his fierce warrior majesty had morphed into
boyish delight as he and Bridie danced in the soak-
ing rain. Hand in hand, joyous and free—he looked
so happy he couldn't stand to look at it for fear of
that feeling being ripped from him.

He hated it.

He couldn't stop looking at it.

At Bridie, incandescently beautiful and tuned so
finely towards the storm and to him, sharing her
joy with him. Two seconds later she'd been sharing
her body with him, swapping kisses, greedy hands
on rain-slicked skin, tasting and taking. The mem-

ory played out while he stood there and stared. No thought for his current surroundings or the image he might be presenting when faced with his unshielded self.

He hated it.

He wanted it gone. 'Take it down.'

'But, Mr Blake… May I call you Judah?'

'No.'

'Mr Blake, I have no intention of bringing ladders and staff out and taking that picture down *now*. Let's talk again tomorrow.'

'Talk about what?'

It was a measure of his preoccupation with the photograph that he hadn't sensed Bridie's approach. She spoke lightly, with an undercurrent of anxiousness in her voice. Her eyes held the same wariness, along with a plea for him to be okay with her exposing them for all to see.

'You said there was a picture of me in the exhibition. You said nothing about hanging a picture of *us*.'

'I thought—'

'Wrong, Bridie. You thought wrong. I do *not* give my permission for you to show this here. I have not given my permission, do you understand?'

'Mr Blake—'

That was his name. He turned towards the gallery owner and made his position perfectly clear. 'Cover it up or take it down. Those are your choices.'

'Judah—'

'Bridie.' One word, with a world of warning behind it. 'I'm offering you a very simple solution, because I like to think I'm a very reasonable man.'

Her jaw firmed, as if she wanted to disagree with him. 'It's dust and rain and life and growth. It's joy. It's the best photo here.'

'It's *personal*.' Couldn't she see how vulnerable he looked? Didn't she realise how private that moment of welcome and renewal had been to him? How he'd let his guard down just once and let her—and only her—see his weakness? 'There is no other place on this earth that I can be me, except for out there. And you want me to share that with strangers?'

He couldn't.

She was asking too much.

'Mr Blake, Bridie, much as I love a good scandal, I really do recommend you set your differences aside for the next hour or two and concentrate on selling art. Red dot on the wall here, see? We can take this picture down tomorrow and when asked, I can say it's at the request of the buyer that it no longer be shown and that this is why collectors should come along to see new works on opening night. This particular piece is *not* part of any marketing material. It's not catalogued online. One night and gone, and for anyone here tonight it will be nothing but a faint memory. Unless we make a production out of removing it, and then it'll be a story.'

He hated it when other people sounded entirely reasonable and he still didn't want to agree with them.

'I'm taking silence as consent.' Gallery owner

Sara smiled encouragingly at them both. 'Drinks all round. For this, I'll even break into my private stash. Anyone for a whisky?'

'Okay,' said Bridie swiftly, and come to think of it her face did look kind of pale beneath all her skilfully applied make-up.

He wondered if he looked thunderous. More like a storm about to break than the smiling man in the pictures.

Bridie turned to him. 'Judah, I'm sorry. I am. I never dreamed you'd react this way to a picture of us in the rain. I had no idea.'

Neither had he.

'Don't do anything rash.'

'Avoid split-second decisions.'

'Give yourself time to adjust.'

Once again he'd done none of that and Bridie had paid the price. 'I'm sorry.' He was. 'I'm not a hero. I can't be that exposed.'

She glanced at the photograph and shook her head as if to clear it. 'I wish I could see what you see when you look at that photo. To me, it's everything I want home and happiness to be, and it's beautiful. You're beautiful like that. You're free.'

'Are there any more like it? From that day?'

'Many, many. The cameras took a photo every thirty seconds. It caught everything.' Her chest rose with the strength of the breath she took. 'You're welcome to see them. I can destroy them. I did ask.' Her eyes pleaded with him to agree with her. 'You *knew* you were standing in the frame.

'I'd never show them,' she added. 'And some of them crossed a line and became way too personal, I know that. I just—I didn't think this one did. I did offer to show it to you on the plane. I *knew* I should have made you look.'

'My bad.' She was right. He'd agreed without knowing what he was agreeing to, and that was on him. 'Spur-of-the-moment reaction.' God knew he'd been warned about *them*. 'I'm coming good.'

He still couldn't bring himself to look at the photo again.

'And here we are.' Sara spared him an answer by way of shoving a silver tray with three crystal tumblers full of Scotch under their noses. 'All but one of the works have sold, and the night is still young. A toast.' She raised the last glass. 'To a remarkable new talent and a sell-out exhibition, I'm sure.'

'Really? All but one? Which one?'

Astonishment looked good on Bridie. Not quite as good as...what did she call it? His gaze skittered over the photo on the wall—the part with Bridie in it, whirling against the storm.

'Boots 'n Dust,' answered Sara. 'Bridie, darling, I'm being asked if you take commissions. Come and meet this wonderful couple from South Australia. I believe they own a grazing property down that way. Can you spare her, Mr Blake?'

'I can spare her.'

'You won't leave without me?' asked Bridie.

Why she still wanted him anywhere near her spoke volumes about her lack of alternatives. 'I won't leave without you. I might step outside though.' Let the lack of walls calm him. 'Text me when you want me to come back in.'

'I will.' She leaned up, her lips to his ear. 'I'm really sorry you don't like the photos but, please, please look at them again. Your superhero photo against the storm is stunning. *You're* stunning—all your inner strength and might. As for the one of us, the you in that pic is every bit as bold and beautiful as you are in the other one, and it's exactly what I want for you, whether I'm the one to share it with you or not.

'Happiness and joy, Judah. Because you deserve it.'

CHAPTER SEVEN

IT WAS HARD to feel like a successful landscape photographer when the man walking beside her was so tense and withdrawn. She should have stuck to landscapes, or at the very least forced Judah to look at the pictures she'd added to the exhibition at the last minute. She hadn't meant to hurt him. He probably hadn't meant to hurt her either, with his emphatic objection to the portrait of the two of them, but he had.

Their tentative friendship was withering away in the silence and she had no idea how to resurrect it.

'You're not coming in?' she asked as he stopped at the entrance to the hotel foyer.

'Not yet. Figured I'd walk for a bit.'

'Want some company?' It was a long shot, because every bone in his body suggested that, no, he damn well didn't.

He looked to her boots. 'In those shoes?'

'I have walking shoes upstairs.'

He shrugged, which could mean anything, but he stayed by her side as they returned to the suite, which was still as luxurious as they had left it, only now there was a bottle of champagne, a fruit basket, and chocolates on the dining table, along with a note congratulating her on her resounding opening-night success.

'From the gallery,' she murmured. 'I'll just go change my shoes.'

'Don't bother.'

Right, so he definitely wasn't interested in enduring any more of her company this evening. 'Okay, no. Didn't mean to intrude on the rest of your evening.'

'I meant that tiredness hit me like a hammer on the way up to the suite and what's not to like about the thought of opening a bottle of celebratory champagne and kicking back now that we're here?'

'Oh. Okay.' Four seasons in one day, that was him.

He reached for the bottle of champagne and made short work of opening it. 'Congratulations. You did it. Sold every painting.'

'And managed to hurt you in the process.' Might as well say it.

'I overreacted. Lashed out.'

'Again.' Because he'd done similar at the ball.

'Again.' He poured the champagne and left plenty of room for the bubbles to rise before topping off the glasses and handing one to her. 'I'm not proud of my behaviour.'

'Do you know why you do it?'

'I have a fair idea.'

She waited, and waited some more, and finally he spoke.

'I don't like being vulnerable. In prison...' He set his glass down on the table and looked her in the eye. 'In prison that's not on. You lock down hard and try to become as emotionless as you can. Nothing gets to you. No fear, no anger, no laughter. Nothing. Emotions are private. And now they're all coming out, all those feelings I don't know what to do with any more, and I feel exposed and it's dangerous. *I'm* dangerous when cornered. I need more control.'

She'd wanted him to reveal a few flaws, hadn't she?

Well, he'd just revealed a few monsters. 'And soon you *will* have more control, because you're honest with yourself and you're working on it. It's not a permanent character flaw. You're downright inspirational.'

'You need to get out more.'

'There's nothing wrong with my judgment.'

'I'm sorry,' he said simply. 'For my behaviour at the ball. For my appalling behaviour tonight. You deserve better.'

'Apology accepted.' He was so hard on himself. 'Please. Can't we just relax? Put on some music and take this party to the patio? You can stare out over the water and brood. I can close my eyes and pretend I'm back home dancing beneath the stars where no one can see me.'

'I see you.'

She turned away, suddenly shy about all but inviting him to look at her.

'You look at me, too,' he added.

How could she not? 'I know.'

'Have you ever had a lover before? Or is that too private a question to ask?'

'I'll answer you.' Honesty was important to her. 'No, I haven't.' Twenty-three-year-old virgin, that was her. 'And it's not because I've been waiting around for you to return. I mean, you were older when we were growing up and I might have had a tiny crush on you in my teens, but it wasn't a fixation. You were the hot older boy who lived next door. I think that's normal enough.'

He made a noise that could have meant agreement and she decided to take it as such.

'After you went to prison, my thoughts ran more along the lines that you were part of my world and I wanted you back in it where you belonged. It wasn't a romantic notion. More of a guilt-induced notion.' She put her glass down. She wasn't thirsty any more.

'You were a kid and you needed protection.' Those words were enough to make her look at him again. 'I don't blame you for what happened. Never have.'

A weight she never knew she carried rolled off her shoulders. 'Really?'

'Really. I don't blame your father or your aunt either, for allowing you to come into contact with a charming sociopath hell-bent on possession. Do you blame them?'

'Of course not.'

'Good. So lose the guilt and don't expect my forgiveness. No one made me do anything I didn't want to do, so there's nothing to forgive.'

'Thank you.' She steadied her thoughts. 'I'm grateful for your actions.'

'Don't be,' he said. 'It makes me question what you'll put up with from me.'

'I'm always going to be grateful to you for rescuing me, that's a given.' She turned and leaned against the railing, her hands lightly clasping it on either side of her and her back to the harbour view as she risked locking eyes with him again. 'I'm making good headway when it comes to not thinking of you as a superhero though.'

He laughed, open and honest, and she cherished the sound.

'Do you think we could press a reset button, you and me? Ignore the past. Forget the false engagement, and the way I exposed you tonight, and start over?' she asked.

'We can try.'

She turned to him and held out her hand. 'Hello. I'm Bridie. I'm not real good around people I don't know and I've never had a man in my bed before, but you make me want to.'

He was laughing again. 'Don't lead with that.' But he took her hand in his and stole her breath away with that simple touch. 'I'm Judah. And I would love to take you to bed, but I currently don't trust my control. I can't promise to make your first time what a first time should be. I'm too…greedy.'

'For touch?' He still hadn't let go of her hand.

'For you.'

'I don't suppose you could keep me in mind and let me know when that control of yours returns?'

'I can do that.'

'Will you dance with me?' she murmured. 'I'm a terrible dancer, unless it's raining, and it's not raining, but moonlight and a beautiful harbour might improve my dancing too.'

'It would be my pleasure to see if it does.'

She held his hand as he led her to the centre of the terrace. She closed her eyes the better to feel him as he turned her into his arms. Those powerful thighs of his brushed against hers as they moved and the warmth of his palm settled in the small of her back and held her close. She dropped his hand but only in order to place both hands on his shoulders. His hands now encircled her waist. It was the school formal she'd never had.

She smiled at the innocence of it all and moments later felt his lips brush hers.

Okay, maybe she could open her eyes just a fraction, the better to see his reaction to the kissing.

He was close enough to see the thickness of his lashes and the faint frown between guarded eyes that held a question.

'There's that lack of control,' he murmured.

Oh. She wouldn't have put it like that. 'Can you do it again?' Three times now he'd smiled or laughed and meant it. She was on a roll. 'You know, if we did want to take this to the bedroom, I could always tie you up.' Would he beg her to release him? Would he strain against the ties that bound him? 'How many neck ties did you bring?'

'You want to go from virgin to dominatrix without passing go? That's nuts.' But his eyes flashed fire and the hands around her waist tightened, before deliberately, on his exhale of breath, making their way to her hips. 'Also, we've only just met.'

'I feel as if I've known you for longer,' she said. 'And I'd check in with you. A lot.' Not as if domination was her goal. 'You could direct me.'

Judah groaned.

Still not a no.

'There could be safe words. Traffic-light colours.'

'And cursing,' he muttered.

'Yes, all the curse words. Not a problem.' She smiled brightly.

'You have no idea what you're asking.'

'True.' But he kissed her again and she didn't think it was a no. She closed her eyes and surrendered to the moment as fire ripped through her veins.

'Do it.'

'What?' She hadn't *actually* been expecting a yes.

'Take my clothes off, tie me up, and use me. Let's see what you've got.'

Bridie felt her breath hitch at his gravelly challenge. 'Okay.'

'Okay.'

'Okay,' she echoed again. Now was not the time

for rampant insecurity to make an appearance. She was Bridie Starr of Devil's Kiss station. A talented photographer who'd just held her first sell-out exhibition. An outback woman, bold and resilient—even if it had taken years to claw her way back to where she was today. She could do this. She could slide his jacket from his shoulders and let it fall. She could undo the buttons on his snow-white shirt. After that, she'd be covering new territory. She could improvise.

'You realise you're talking to yourself?' he asked.

'Oh. Did I say all that out loud?'

'Yeah.'

'Sorry about that. Then again…you'll be forewarned.' He smelled so good, so undeniably cologney and male that she couldn't resist putting her nose to the curve of his neck and breathing deeply of his scent and setting her lips to the skin below his ear. This was lovely—having free rein to indulge herself and experiment.

The shudder that ripped through him was encouraging.

'There are ties in my suitcase,' he offered.

'Show me.'

He removed his cufflinks on the way and she might have objected except that following him to his bedroom gave her the most wonderful opportunity to ogle the breadth of his back and the globes of his rear.

He found two ties and held them out to her with an air of challenge that was impossible to resist. She slid them around her neck, where they hung like a dressmaker's tape. She'd get around to using them, as promised. Soon.

First, she had a man to undress.

Bridie's thoroughness was killing him. Slowly, surely, as inevitable as sunset, she built a fire in him that threatened to become an inferno. She finished undoing the buttons of his shirt, and the brush of her fingers and knuckles almost had him coming out of his skin. She pressed a kiss to his chest as she slid the shirt to the floor, and then tilted her head up towards his.

'How am I doing?' Her voice only wobbled a little bit.

'Not bad.'

'Let me just strike *gives effusive praise* off your list of strengths.' But her hands kept exploring and her eyes shone with gentle humour and encouragement.

'Pretty good,' he offered in an effort to redeem himself.

'Funny man. May I kiss you?' Her lips brushed his, more tease than kiss. 'Please?'

'Yes.'

Her next kiss delved deeper, took longer and he couldn't help but take command of it. Showing her how to savour the sweetness, and by the time he'd done a thorough enough job, she'd opened his trousers and he was making tight little sounds of what could have been taken as protest but were far more aligned with surrender.

'Are you sure you want me to tie you? I mean… this is going pretty well.'

He stepped back, but only to take his trousers off, and she looked down and her eyes widened.

'Oh,' she murmured. 'Oh, boy.'

Virgin, his mind supplied helpfully. And he was definitely no boy.

'I should, er—or you should… I mean—' Flailing looked good on her. 'How does that even fit?'

'It fits.'

'Right. Of course. Of course it does. So if you just…lie on the bed and raise your arms and grab a couple of bars on the bedhead, I'll, wow, okay, that's a lot of muscle mass. How strong is a brass bedhead, do you think?'

He curled his hands around two rounded bedhead rails and figured them for hollow. 'I'll replace it if I have to.'

'How very reassuring.'

'Tie me up, Bridie. Do it now.' Before raging need got the better of him and he reached for her and forgot to be gentle. He wasn't even sure he knew how to be gentle these days. It was as if he had two settings: indifferent or destructive. The middle ground had deserted him.

She straddled him to do it, but instead of resting any weight on him she held herself a couple of inches above him. Suddenly his hands were on her hips, pulling her down against him before she could squeak. Silk panties, warm and slippery against his sensitised skin, meant he almost lost it.

Forget his overwhelming hunger for sex and how it might scare her. He needed in.

Needed to push aside her panties and sink into tight, willing warmth.

'No, you don't.' She reached for one of his wrists and slid a loop of fabric over his hand and pulled it tight and then raised his arm to the bedhead again. 'Co-operate,' she murmured, and he gave in to the urge to bury his face against the softness of her belly and surround himself with her scent.

'I am co-operating.' His voice was muffled but he trusted her to understand. He hadn't ripped her panties off, rolled her onto her back and buried himself inside her yet. How could she possibly think he wasn't co-operating?

She tied his other hand to the bedhead and smiled as she sat back and set the palms of her hands to his chest.

'Sit,' he urged. 'Make yourself comfortable.' He almost whimpered when she removed herself from the bed altogether, but it was only to raise her top over her head. 'Or that. Do that.'

Champagne-coloured lace underwear worked for him, no doubt, and for a moment he thought she'd get rid of that too and be as naked as him, but at the last minute she seemed to think better of it.

She was all long lines and slender curves and he wanted more.

This was torture.

'Music?' She made it happen, and then returned and knelt on the bed next to him as her gaze roved over him. 'May I touch you?'

Sometime this century would be good. 'Yes.'

She started at his fingertips, a slow, thorough investigation of every inch of him until she reached the planes and ridges of his stomach. Goosebumps followed in her wake and he closed his eyes and let his passion soar. He felt her hair brush his stomach before he felt her lips.

'Is this okay?'

'Don't stop.' *Never, ever stop.*

Eyes closed, he wasn't ready for the tentative lick she bestowed on the tip of his hard length. He should have strapped his feet to the bed too, because he'd follow that warm mouth to the ceiling if it meant he could have more of it. He clenched his hands around the ties that bound him and tried not to fill her mouth with more. Her pace, not his. Bridie in control.

By the time she'd explored every part of his erection with hands and mouth, his dignity had been shredded and the sounds coming out of him had more in common with beast than man.

'I'm not protected,' she murmured.

'Bathroom. Bottom drawer. Hotel supplies.' Bless them.

Her leaving the room gave him time to claw back slim threads of control.

'Large, Extra Large and Jumbo,' she murmured

as she sank back down on the bed with a handful of condoms. 'I'm guessing now is not the time for social commentary on condom marketing?'

'So not the time.'

'Jumbo?'

'Yeah.' And even that would be a stretch. 'Roll it on me, sit on my stomach and lean towards me.' Would she do it? Take blunt direction from him?

Yes.

He tried to be gentle with her as he traced the contours of her bra with his lips. When he tongued a pebbled nipple and then closed his mouth over it and sucked gently, silk and all, she fed him more and caught her breath. *Yes.*

'More,' she whispered.

He'd have headed south, but Bridie wanted more kisses. This was why he was tied up and she was running this.

And then she dropped her panties and shed her bra and sat right back down with her soft folds caressing his length, and he dug his heels in and bucked. No need for anything to go in yet. 'Rock it, yes. Like that.'

He set up a slow rolling grind to help her find her way. He was already well on his way to insanity born of unutterable need as their kisses grew wilder and a storm rose within him. Bound, stripped bare, and aching for every little piece of her she was willing to give. So good. Beyond anything he'd ever experienced.

And then she changed the angle of her hips and he nudged her entrance and eased the very tip of him in. He all but howled his approval.

'Oh, you like that?'

Queen of understatement. She did it again, took him in hand and tested for fit, and he stilled on an upstroke, his teeth bared and his lips tight, so close to coming he could hardly bear it.

Had his hands been free… But they weren't and he was glad of it. 'More, Bridie, please. Just…use me.'

'I— It's…' She slid him a fraction further in and he met resistance.

'Perfect?' A man could hope.

'Daunting.'

'Give me your breasts again.' Maybe it'd help. This time he wasn't quite as careful. Laving became grazing, teasing turned to sucking. Bridie took more of him in and it was all he could do to stay still and not rear up and take what she seemed so determined to give.

It wasn't enough. She was hurting, not soaring. Curses left his lips as he pleaded for her to untie him so he could see to her pleasure, and his, but she refused him. His thrusting grew wilder and she stayed with him, getting looser, he thought, or maybe he only imagined she did. Her breathing grew ragged and she broke kisses in an effort to draw breath.

He came when she dug her nails into his chest. Nothing he could do about it other than dig his heels in and take his pleasure and strain and demand that she untie him.

Not until he softened inside her did she reach for the ties at his wrists. 'You bent the bedhead,' she said, but he barely heard her as he exploded into action, rolling her onto her back and getting his mouth between her legs, ravenous and apologetic for letting his pleasure come before hers.

He found her nub and set about driving her as insane as she'd so recently driven him. Inhibition had long ago left him as he set up a rough, pulsing rhythm, using his fingers to expose her and his mouth and tongue to bring her to completion. Satisfaction savaged him as she wove her hands through his hair, her eyes half hidden between generous lashes. He slid his hands beneath her buttocks, the better to position her, and figured he could stay there for ever.

She came on his tongue moments later, flooding him with sweetness, delighting him with her responsiveness.

He who hadn't held or been held in years allowed her to lead him back up the bed. 'You okay?' she asked. It nearly broke him. He didn't deserve such tenderness.

She checked his wrists and kissed the redness, a question in her eyes.

'It's nothing,' he said.

She tucked in beside him, with her head on his shoulder and her hand to his chest as if she belonged there, and he was powerless against her expectations. 'Are you okay?' he finally asked.

'I'm brilliant,' she murmured on the edge of sleep. 'Best night ever.'

So easy to please.

She'd wanted what he had to offer. She was happy with him, demons and all.

Wasn't that something?

CHAPTER EIGHT

BRIDIE WOKE THE next morning, tucked up against the hard, warm body of a sleeping man whose chest rose and fell in a slow, even rhythm. He'd turned into her at some point during the night, and how he could even breathe with her hair in his face was a miracle, but he managed it. She turned, little spoon to his big one, step one of her exit plan, and stared out through the floor-to-ceiling window at the sky, before closing her eyes and savouring the feel of skin against skin.

Morning could wait just that little bit longer, couldn't it?

Morning would mean conversation and explanation. Justification of actions that needed no justification and everything would become awkward again.

Her body ached in places it never had before, but she welcomed the feeling.

Welcome to sex, Bridie. Any complaints?

Not a one, except maybe her partner insisting he be tied up so he didn't get too rowdy for her. He hadn't. When she'd freed his hands he'd turned all that intense passion and power on her and sent her straight to heaven.

He hadn't left her during the night to go walking the streets or sleep under the night sky or whatever it was that he usually did. He'd stayed with her.

It was a heady, welcome thought given that her desire for him hadn't faded one little bit. She could go again. Her body was still stretched and moist for him. Unless… She teased her entrance with gentle fingers and felt no pain, but it was mighty damp, and when she saw her fingers they were red, and…

Oh.

Shower. Now.

Before Judah woke up and decided he'd split her in two.

She sprang from the bed and hightailed it to the bathroom and he let her go, not a word of protest and no physical restraint, and she didn't look back to see if she'd woken him. She was too busy being embarrassed.

Not until she'd washed away all evidence of last night's lovemaking did she lift her face to the spray. Was there a way to sneak back into bed with him after her hasty exit? A casual word or two: toilet break, now, where were we? Did she have the confidence for that?

Probably not.

She dressed and called for coffee and breakfast to be delivered. Same coffee orders as yesterday, full breakfast for two, and by the time it arrived and the concierge had arranged it on the table, Judah had appeared in the doorway.

'I ordered for us. Hope you don't mind.'

'I don't mind.'

He padded forward to take his coffee, his body honed for battle and his expression guarded. 'You left.'

'The bathroom was calling. Loudly.'

He studied her over the rim of his coffee cup. 'And you didn't return.'

'But I was just about to come in and try and wake you with the smell of good coffee.' There was that.

'Did I hurt you last night?'

He just wouldn't let it go. 'Physically, no. Though I'm a little sad that I've wasted so many years not having sex, because *damn*, Judah. I loved it.'

She had the pleasure of watching a slow blush steal across his cheeks. 'Oh, really?'

'Flat-out loved it.' Where were her manners? 'Thank you for the introduction. Although I'm sure I still have so much to learn.'

No offer to tutor her was forthcoming. But he did raise an eyebrow and hold her gaze.

She was Bridie from the bush and so many of its hazards didn't faze her. Surely she could continue her line of reasoning in the face of a raised eyebrow. 'You didn't overwhelm me. You could teach me. You could use hands.' Was that a flash of amusement in his eyes? Hard to tell, it was gone so quickly, leaving careful blankness in its wake. 'I'm sensing you have regrets.'

'Don't you?' he asked.

'Not one. Haven't you been listening?'

'You're in a hotel room with a man who made you tie him to the bed before he'd have sex with you. I'm wondering why you haven't fled.'

'Because it's you, and you had…reasons.' She waved a hand around to approximate those reasons. 'And I trust you.' Surely that was a good thing?

But he didn't seem to be similarly ecstatic about her confidence in him. Matter of fact, he looked downright uncomfortable. 'But I can take no for an answer, if it wasn't that good for you and you never want to do it again. Paradise lost and all that.' And on to breakfast before she fell apart in front of him. 'We have mushroom, bean sprout and three-cheese omelettes, bacon on the side, tropical fruits, yoghurt, and everything else on the menu that we don't usually have access to at home.' She lifted domes from plates as she spoke. 'Dig in.'

Maybe she'd done something right, because that was an invitation he didn't refuse and boy could he pack it away. She was more of a grazer, not all that food-focused, whereas he went for it to the extent that she wondered if he ever got full. He caught her watching, and she looked away, but not before he'd downed his utensils and pushed his plate aside with an abruptness that scraped along the tabletop and every nerve she owned.

She didn't know what to say. 'More coffee? I think it's a two-coffee kind of morning.'

His nod was enough to get her heading for the phone to order it. 'Anything else?'

'No.'

She didn't press. 'When's checkout?'

'Twelve.'

With their flight at five. They had all morning to fill in.

'Do you need to go back to the gallery this morning?' he asked.

Conversation initiated by him. She'd take it. 'Yes. Probably a good move to make sure the print you don't want on display comes home with us. Or goes home with you. Or me. Or whatever you want.' Was there any ground between them that wasn't treacherous? If there was, she hadn't found it yet. 'I do want to check out the button shop near the opal shop if I have the time.'

'Button shop,' he echoed. 'Because you need buttons?'

'No, I've just never been in a button shop before. Want to come along?'

'No.'

And why would he? He might have been sitting opposite her at the breakfast table, but every word, every look, spoke of a distance he wanted to maintain. Whatever they'd done together last night, however much his body had betrayed him, he seemed driven to regain control. And control was fine, he could have it, but did it really have to come with such distance between them?

'You're kind of remote this morning. I'm not sure what I was expecting.' But it wasn't this level of awkwardness. 'Hugs?' She was rewarded with a blank stare, but soldiered on regardless. Last night she'd asked for what she wanted and received it. The strategy bore repeating. 'Kisses?'

His gaze dropped to her fingers, her wedding-ring finger in particular, and he frowned.

Oh. The ring. Right. 'It's not as if I'm suddenly expecting our engagement to become real,' she sought to assure him. 'We still have a plan to end it, and I know it's not real and there'll come a time when…oh!' Man, she was so *stupid*. 'Last night at the gallery when we argued in public… Do you want to use it to set the scene for our break-up? Because that makes sense.' Of course it did. And here she was, begging for good-morning kisses.

The melon on her plate lost all appeal, nothing but slimy squares of food she doubted she'd be able to swallow. 'When do you want to do it? Today?' She reached for the engagement ring on her finger. Why was she even wearing it when she wasn't in public? It hadn't been genuinely given. Judah definitely didn't want to spend the rest of his days with her—he could barely manage a weekend. One night had been enough for him. A night out of time. No repeats. 'I'm sorry.' It wouldn't come off.

'Bridie—'

'It does come off, bear with. I don't want to damage it.' Her clammy hands and fumbling fingers weren't co-operating.

'*Bridie.*' She'd given him the perfect excuse to pull back, so why did he reach out to cover her hands and stop her from removing his ring? Why did her panic soothe him? Make him feel even more tuned into her than he had been last night? Did he feel better for knowing she was even more vulnerable than him? What kind of person did that make him?

The way out of this crazy engagement was right there in front of him. He had his land back and had paid Bridie fair market price for it. The Conrad place was his. He'd been there for her when she'd launched her new career. He'd made a mistake and had done his best to limit the fallout for them both. He could end this farce of an engagement here and now and *finish* this. Minimise the damage he was doing to her. So, why didn't he just let her take the ring off and give it back to him?

It wasn't chivalry that made him reach out and close his hand over hers. He just wanted that ring to stay right where it was. 'Stop,' he ordered gently. 'Let's not do that today. We'll get around to it eventually, and when we do we'll be ready with press statements, business goals in place and a story about how we make much better business partners than lovers.'

She stilled and searched his face as if testing his sincerity, so he gave it to her and to hell with the consequences.

'As for last night…' She bit her lip and let him continue. 'I didn't do right by you last night.'

'By all means, make it up to me.'

Her enthusiasm was so good for his ego. 'I intend to. What kind of jewellery do you like?'

'Are you going to buy your way out of a hole every time you think you don't measure up?'

Was that what he was doing? 'It's an option.'

'No, it's not.' She seemed adamant. 'Not with me. If you want to put last night behind us and never do it again, just say so. I'm tough. I can take it.'

So *not tough*. He remained terrified he would do something wrong by accident and break her. 'I do want to continue having sex with you. That's a given. But I'm also expecting you to give up on me eventually, and I don't blame you. Until then have at me.'

She sat back, eyes narrowed. What had he done now? No split-second decision-making here—he was thinking hard about how a relationship between them would eventually play out.

'No hard feelings,' he added.

'That's not the point, Judah. The point is to *have* all the feelings! You walked out here this morning and you've shut all yours back down!'

'Not all of them.' Frustration was riding him pretty hard at the moment. 'If you want an open, fun-loving guy who's in touch with his emotions, *that's not me*. It might never be me. *This* is the real me. Take a good long look.'

Who could blame her if she walked away?

She pulled her hand out from beneath his and aimed a smile at him that missed by a mile. 'You're such an ass. And if you think I'm ever going to give up on you, you don't know me. Lovers or not.'

They glared at one another across the table. Bridie was the first to break. 'I'm going button shopping.'

Buttons. This whole conversation had started with buttons. It was enough to make a zip man out of him. 'Let's meet for lunch. Fresh seafood. Outdoors.'

She stood. 'Is it a date or am I back to being your neighbour and fake fiancée again?'

'It's a date.'

'Good.'

She was almost to her bedroom door. 'Bridie—'

Make that through the bedroom door and out of sight. 'The sex was good. Better than good.' He'd damn near torn his hands from his wrists with the force of his ecstasy, and practically passed out afterwards. 'Thank you for putting up with me. For keeping us safe.'

Her head appeared from the other side of the doorframe, a riot of golden autumn curls and sparkly hoop earrings. Her eyes were guarded; he'd put that look there and that was a good thing. And then she smiled, and he could have sworn the sun came out. 'I loved it too.'

He was so screwed.

CHAPTER NINE

THE BUTTON SHOP Bridie ended up visiting supplied all
the costume needs of major theatre groups in Sydney.
Vintage buttons were especially amazing, Bridie had
a sold-out exhibition on her hands and three landscape commission enquiries and the write-up on the
show was headed for the weekend magazine of the
national daily newspaper, courtesy of the 'palpable
tension and dramatic history between two scions of
the Australian outback community'.

'I can't control what photos will be used, but with
a headline like that you can bet the story will make
mention of the work Mr Blake wanted removed,'
Sara had told her bluntly. 'I realise that won't go
down well with him.'

'Can you ask them not to?'

'I can. You or Mr Blake might have better luck
with that.'

Bridie didn't look forward to letting Judah know.
'You pulled the picture from the exhibition?'

The older woman nodded. 'Where would you like
it sent. Also, framed or unframed?'

'I'll take it with me now, unframed. Thank you so much.'

'And is Mr Blake in…better spirits this morning?'

'Yes. He's quite recovered.'

'If you ever become worried for your safety, *call* me. Or come here to the gallery. I know the drill and I know it intimately. I can help you.'

Bridie blinked, taken aback. Did worldly, sophisticated Sara honestly believe that Judah would hurt her? On the strength of his behaviour last night? It hadn't been that bad, had it? 'Oh, wow, *no*. Sara, I appreciate your offer but you have it all wrong. I trust Judah with my life and for very good reason.'

'Of course, of course you do.' Sara's words flowed like redirected water. 'But my offer still stands. Call any time, and if you start talking about an imaginary exhibition in, say, London, I'll know you need help.'

'Okay.' What else could she say? 'Is this because of Judah's past? His reputation?'

'No, it's because I'm a woman of a certain age, with a lot of experience, and I lose nothing by mentioning that I am here for you if ever you need a safe place to be.' Sara gestured for Bridie to walk with her towards the office area. 'Now. Let's talk about booking you for another show.'

Judah was waiting for her when she stepped from the gallery. Only innate grace kept Bridie from stumbling down the stairs at the sight of him. 'Are you waiting for me?'

'Yes.'

'Because of this?' She held up the art tube containing the picture of them. 'Because it's right here.' She handed it to him without any more ceremony. 'The bad news is that the write-up in this weekend's paper is likely to mention it, and they're going to rake up our past connections as well as our present ones, which… I guess I expected that. Did you?'

'Of course.' He began to walk towards the quay, same direction as the hotel. 'But apart from that the write-up is good?'

'Sara thinks it will be.'

'Good. I have a water taxi ordered for half eleven. It'll take us to a restaurant the concierge recommended.'

But when they got to the hotel and he'd handed the picture tube over to be taken to the room, he steered her towards the tiny jewellery cubby to the left of the foyer. It had a three-strand pearl necklace and diamond and pearl earrings on a black dummy's bust in the window and was so beautifully lit that it looked like a renaissance painting. The pearls glowed with a magical lustre and the lack of anything resembling a price tag suggested that budget-conscious shoppers should keep on walking.

'C'mon in, I want your advice on something.' He opened the jewellery shop door and held it for her.

Was he buying something for himself?

'Mr Blake.' The gentleman behind the counter beamed.

Judah nodded. 'Martin. This is Miss Starr.'

'Enchanted.' The man reached below the counter and lifted up a velvet pad that contained three necklaces, clearly designed for women. Bridie looked to Judah.

'For you,' he said. 'A gift from me.'

She hadn't forgotten his earlier words about buying her jewellery because he felt he'd let her down somehow.

He hadn't.

His brutal honesty—in everything he said and did—was a gift in itself, forcing her to examine her own behaviour and immaturity. 'You don't have to. This weekend is already...' she shrugged a little helplessly '...gorgeous. Thought provoking. Revealing.'

'All the more reason for you to have something to remember it by. Take a look. I don't know your taste. You might not like any of them.'

But that wasn't the problem, because she loved all of them. The problem was the no-doubt astronomical and currently invisible price tags that accompanied the necklaces.

'I can't.' She backed up until she hit the door.

'A photo a month. A lifeline to home. You gave me that.' He nodded towards the counter. 'They don't even compare. Trinkets.'

'Beautiful, expensive trinkets,' she corrected as she met the salesman's long-suffering smile.

'Thank you, Miss Starr. Yes, yes, they are all beautiful and expensive, although I can't quite bring myself to call them trinkets—even if the customer is always right,' said Martin the despairing salesman, before regrouping. 'Take this one, for example: a triplet of perfectly graded natural white South Sea pearls with a nineteen-carat fire opal centrepiece set in platinum. A classic design.'

'Gorgeous.' She admired it from afar. 'Not exactly something you'd wear every day.'

'No indeed, Miss Starr. That one's a statement trinket.' He moved on to the next necklace, lifting it and letting it dangle from his fingers. '*This* one you could wear every day.'

Maybe if you were a queen. Or, nope, not even then. Bridie eyed the diamond and sapphire art deco pendant, before turning to look at Judah. 'Are you serious?'

'Do I not look serious?' He had a smile in his eyes that was hard to resist. 'I like the third one.'

It was a modern piece. A swirling landscape of white diamonds, black pearls, cerulean sapphires and pinky-orange-coloured stones that glowed with no less dazzle than the diamonds and sapphires. 'What are the pinkish stones?'

'Padparadscha sapphires, ethically mined, of course. Aren't they wonderful?'

'Stunning.' She leaned closer and the salesman mirrored her. 'But still not an everyday wearer.'

The man spread his hands, his expression helpless. 'Madam, we don't *do* everyday wearers.'

'She'll take that one,' said Judah, and to her, 'Today's a good day. Wear it to lunch.'

So she wore it to lunch and tossed her head and felt like a million dollars as she collected admiring gazes from nearby strangers. Maybe it was the pendant they were looking at. Maybe it was Judah, handsome sod with a watchful quality about him and a stare that encouraged people to mind their own business.

But even he couldn't resist the glitter of the harbour and a playful breeze, a cold beer at his fingertips and the freshest of seafood.

'I could do this more often,' she told him with a deep sense of satisfaction.

'Glad to hear it.'

'What about you? Enjoying yourself? Because you get all flinty eyed every so often.'

'Is that so?'

'Yeah. Seagulls giving you trouble?'

'More like some of your admirers don't know when to stop staring.'

Ah.

'Do you get that a lot?'

She nodded. 'And I've never enjoyed that kind of attention, but it's what you get with a face like mine. Beauty has its price. Or they could be trying to put a price on my absolutely stunning necklace.'

'Suits you,' he rumbled. 'Why have you stayed single when you could have any man you want?'

'Trust issues, I guess. Past trauma. Former shut-in. I might look like the prettiest doll in the shop but the hidden damage does run deep. And I live in the middle of nowhere—and like it.' She narrowed her gaze. 'I wasn't waiting for you, if that's what you're getting at. I thought I covered that last night.'

'You did.'

'And I know you're probably going to tire of me, because once you do adjust to life outside you'll shine so bright you'll leave me behind. But I'm aiming to enjoy you while I have you. I like you. I trust you. It's enough.' It had to be enough. He wasn't offering anything else and she was okay with that.

Mostly.

'Who else do you trust?' he asked.

'My father, Gert, Reid, my aunt—even though she thinks she failed me. That's five. Not bad. What about you? Who do you trust?'

He shrugged and lifted his beer to his lips.

'Anyone?' She waited for him to answer, but it was a long wait. 'Not even Reid?'

'He's young.'

'He's loyal,' she stressed. 'Give him a chance.' *And me,* she refrained from saying. *Give me a chance too. I'll do my best by you.*

But he didn't need that kind of pressure and neither did she. Maybe all they needed to do was take everything one moment at a time. 'I'm having fun. Are you having fun?'

'Maybe I am.'

'Oh, go on, say yes and make my day. I like where

we're sitting, by the way. Both of us with our backs against the wall so we can see what's going on. In feng shui they call this the command position.'

'Is that so?'

'Yup. I'm a fount of useless information.'

'Good to know. How was the button shop?'

'Brilliant. Buttons have stories. I bought blue ones.'

'I can barely order from a menu, there's so much choice,' he offered after a moment. 'A button store would have blown my mind.'

From teasing to serious information in the space of a heartbeat. *Pay attention, Bridie, to what this man chooses to share.* 'Were you always like that with choices?' she asked carefully, and he shook his head.

'No. In prison they take choices away. Stay there long enough and *not* making choices becomes the norm.'

'But you're making all sorts of big business deci-sions. Huge, important ones with far-reaching con-sequences for conservation and land management. How does that fit?'

'That's something I've been thinking about since my teens and I've had plenty of time to fine-tune those dreams. There's money there to do it and mak-ing it happen is easy. There's no oysters versus br-uschetta decision on the table.'

It didn't make sense to her, but it clearly made sense to him. 'I'd be impressed by your ability to compartmentalise except that eccentric billionaires are a dime a dozen.'

'We are not!'

'Maybe not,' she conceded with a grin. 'And thank you for telling me about your button issues. I like that you did.'

He looked oddly shy for a moment. 'You wanted to get to know me.'

'I still do. And when it comes to your land conservation plans, I want to help. I literally have tens of thousands of landscape and wildlife photos you can use in marketing or promo campaigns, and I'm up for taking more specific shots if you need them.'

'Just don't make me choose which ones.'

'I won't. Those decisions can be mine all mine.'

Look at us, she thought, all smiley and compatible. Take that, weekend headlines. What palpable tension and dramatic history between them? 'If I order the orange and almond cake and you order the sticky date pudding, I can try both of my favourite desserts on this menu. Not that I'm greedy and entitled, but I may just be an opportunist. Are you in?'

His smile came swiftly and, she liked to think, appreciatively. The shaking of his head suggested no, but then, 'Yeah,' he said. 'I'm in.'

By the time they arrived home that night a new understanding had sprung up between them.

No more pretending to be strong and invulnerable for either of them. Eccentricities were welcome—between them they had a fine selection—and upon request they would take a stab at explaining where they came from.

Trust didn't come easily to Bridie, but regardless of what had happened this weekend she still trusted him.

As for Judah's trust in her, Bridie figured he'd made some small headway with that this weekend, what with all she'd learned about him. They weren't friends—sorry, Reid, not a chance in hell, what with the sexy bondage times and the jewellery fit for a princess, not to mention all the button talk.

But they were something.

CHAPTER TEN

'WHAT HAVE YOU done to my brother?'

Reid stood on her veranda, hands on his hips and the dust from his buzzbox helicopter settling into every crack and crevice and on every surface it could find. 'How many times do I have to tell you?' she muttered sternly, and tried to look mean and ornery from her spot at the kitchen door. 'No helicopters in the home paddock. And what do you mean what have I done to your brother? I am his friend. I listen when he speaks, argue with him on occasion and try to keep up with the way he thinks.'

She'd also made it abundantly clear that he was welcome in her bed at any time, but so far he hadn't taken her up on that invitation.

'He's up at five every morning for push-ups and a workout, and then there's the daily meal menu—deviate from that at your peril—and then he has meetings until one, and every day he makes a point of grabbing me to watch the sun set and to tell me what he's been doing in as few words as possible. Yesterday his exact words were "I just bought a demo salt pond power plant to our west, and now I want all the land in between as well." Millions and millions of dollars' worth of deals, just like that.'

'Really not seeing your problem. Your brother's a powerhouse who now owns a powerhouse. Embrace it.'

'He still doesn't sleep in his bed.'

'Ah.' Sometimes he came to visit Bridie and told her all sorts of things about his hopes and dreams and what he wanted to achieve. Sometimes he took a stack of her print photos and took himself out to the veranda and laid them all out and then spent a good hour or more choosing his favourite.

She'd come to learn that it didn't really matter if there was something drastically wrong with the picture he chose. Celebration lay in the fact that he'd managed to choose one.

Sometimes he spent the night on the daybed on her veranda. But he spent it alone and come morning he'd be gone, with nothing to show that he'd ever been there in the first place, except that one time when a generous handful of paper daisies had appeared outside the French doors that led from the veranda to her bedroom.

If they now took pride of place in a cut crystal vase on the top of her bedroom chest of drawers, that was her business.

'Your brother's healing. He's finding himself and making up for lost time and doing a brilliant job of it. Be proud of him.'

Reid threw his hands up in surrender. 'You are so utterly gone on him.'

'Am not.'

'Are too. Last night he stripped the house of every item of green clothing, including mine, and now I can't find my best jacket.'

And he never would. 'The jacket is gone. Sacrificed to last night's bonfire. Something to do with never wanting to wear or see prison greens ever again.'

'It was my favourite jacket!'

'Have you tried wearing more pink?' She had. 'Or yellow? Or bright florals? Because you can probably influence your brother by colour alone, but don't tell him I said that. It's my secret weapon. Oh, and if you're looking for bath towels there's more coming. I ordered them this morning. Very colourful. Lots of spots and pretty patterns.'

'We already have a million bath towels,' Reid muttered as he stomped up the steps.

'Had,' she corrected. 'Apparently they were threadbare, or white gone grey, or something.' It really had been a magnificent bonfire. Very cathartic.

'Aargh!' Unlike his brother, Reid wasn't slow to let his emotions out. 'Why are you enabling him? I'll have no clothes left! There is eccentric and then there is Judah!'

There was some slight…more than slight…truth to Reid's words. 'Want some coffee? I have freshly baked Anzac biscuits for dunking?'

'I hope they're the size of dinner plates. I'm in a mood.'

'Yes. Yes, you are.' This earned her a teenage glare.

Reid was almost as at home in her kitchen as she was. She put the biscuits in front of him and turned to sort out the coffee. He'd straddle the bald blue chair with the fence paling backrest and scratch at the paint, the way he always did. The chair sat directly opposite the wood-fire stove that only got fired up in the deepest of winter nights. It didn't matter that fire so rarely burned in it. He was ready for it.

Judah wasn't the only eccentric Blake on the planet. Maybe it was a displaced Englishman thing.

'He's hired a home office assistant bookkeeper person, sight unseen,' said Reid as she put hot coffee in an oversized mug on the counter beside him. 'She's twenty-two, been in the foster care system since her father went to prison when she was ten, and she never finished school.' He pointed his Anzac biscuit in her direction. 'Let's hope she doesn't like wearing green.'

An office assistant? This was not altogether welcome news. 'Where's she going to live?'

'Shearer's quarters.'

'For how long?'

'Ask your colour censorship partner in crime. And while you're at it, remind him that his brother is not a kid and should be part of the hiring process next time, with a voice and a vote and a *say* in who gets to live in his back yard.'

'You're right. I'll tell him all that.' She didn't know what to think about another woman living out here and working closely with Judah. What if he came to like her? What if he sought out Bridie less?

'Whatever you're planning, I like it,' said Reid, watching her closely.

'I have no idea what you're talking about.' She schooled her expression into something a little less murderous.

'You don't fool me. You're shook too.'

'What is this shook? I'm good with change these days. Change is inevitable.'

'I'm glad you think so, because I'm going to Townsville this afternoon to collect our new employee. Want me to get anything for you while I'm there?'

Now that he mentioned it... 'Fresh pearl perch, a dozen rock oysters, black caviar, two lemons and a lettuce that doesn't need resuscitation.'

He stood up and swung the chair he'd been sitting on around the right way.

'If you can have it waiting for collection at hangar two, you've got it. Tell them to leave it in the cold room,' he said.

'I adore you.'

'I'm counting on it. Tell Judah I have one very nice, very olive-green woollen jumper left. Mum knitted it. When I wear it it's like a hug from someone who's just not there any more, do you know what

I mean? I can't lose it. Can you make him understand that?'

'Why can't you tell him that?'

'Every time I mention the parents he shuts me
down. He's not talking about them, which means I
don't get to either.'

Her heart went out to him. Shades of her father,
who never ever mentioned her mother because the
pain was too vast. 'I'll tell him.' That was a promise. 'And I'll make him understand.'

Judah liked to think he stood still for no one, but the
sight of Bridie lit by firelight demanded he halt and
commit that vision to memory. Why else did he have
so many bonfires at her place? He was running out of
things to burn. Tonight, though…tonight she'd met
him at her kitchen door in a pink slip of a dress that
made him want to reach out and stroke every bit of
her with reverent hands.

Reid had brought an esky full of fresh seafood
back for Bridie, at Bridie's request, and Bridie had
needed someone to eat it with. Reid was busy settling the new girl in, so Judah was it.

That was how Bridie had put the invitation to
him, and apart from a slight curtness in her voice
that he couldn't quite pin down to anything in particular, he'd taken her invitation at face value and
rocked up showered, shaved, dressed for dinner and
in a good mood.

Decision-making skills were coming back to him.

He didn't expect oysters, caviar and his choice of beer or champagne to be waiting for him inside the formal dining room of Starr homestead, but it was. Candlelight too and pressed tin ceiling painted duck-egg blue, with the walls a deeper blue altogether, wooden baseboards and an open fireplace up one end. Had it been winter, it might have been lit but at the moment it was stacked with wine. Photos of her parents and a pair of tall blue vases sat on the mantel. A spectacular black-and-white photo of channel country hung on the wall. He didn't need to ask in order to know that it was one of hers.

She'd gone to a lot of trouble to feed them this evening and, even if he didn't know why, he wasn't ungrateful.

He looked to the scarred oak dining table. Lots of glassware, lots of cutlery and, given his family history and schooling, he automatically knew what to do with every bit of it, no decision making required.

It wasn't until he pulled her chair out and saw her seated that he spotted the engagement ring and bracelet he'd given her months ago winking at him from the centre of the scarred oak dining room table. He took a deep breath and let it out slowly and hopefully silently as he took a vicelike grip on his composure. Don't jump to conclusions. *Don't* make snap decisions. No one went to this much trouble in order to break a fake engagement. Not that he had any experience with that. 'What's this?'

'*This* is a reckoning.' She swept a bare hand towards the table, urging him to sit. 'Either way, we're celebrating a productive few months and your outstanding re-entry into society.'

Pretty words and possibly true, but there was a pile of his family jewels sitting on the table and he couldn't quite let that go. 'What kind of a reckoning?'

'A long overdue one, according to my libido. Sit, eat.' She leaned forward and lit a candelabra full of candles and snared him twice over with her beauty. He'd gained a lot of knowledge these past few weeks, months, plenty of it to do with his neighbour, friend and false fiancée, Bridie. She was resourceful and smart. Playful. Sneaky, even. Her father was still not home and she'd taken control of Devil's Kiss station with a sure and steady hand.

No doubt about it, Bridie Starr was an extraordinarily capable woman when on her home turf, and especially when she had a camera in her hand.

Time to pay attention.

'What do you want?' He asked more plainly. 'Because if you're looking for permission to show the pictures you took of me the other day, the answer is no. Hell no.' He'd been cleaning out a water trough for the cattle with his hat, and he'd taken his shirt off because why get that soaked too, and somehow he'd broken the water stopper while he was at it, which meant he was in there, boots and all with a fix, and by the end of it, he'd just laid back and closed his eyes and let the damn trough fill with him in it, his arms trailing over the edges and his wet hat back on his head.

'No,' he'd said when he'd heard her camera start clicking, but he hadn't really meant it and he'd been too content to move.

'But, Judah, *Man in Bath*,' she'd muttered and somehow managed to capitalise every word, and then she'd started *positioning* him.

He'd given her plenty of warning to put the camera down before dragging her in with him.

'I would *never* again put any of the pictures I take of you out in the world for public viewing. Lesson learnt.' Her hand over her heart only served to highlight the necklace snugged against the gentle swell of her breasts. *His* necklace, the one he'd pressured her into accepting. He hadn't seen it on her since they'd left Sydney. What was it the sales guy had said? Not a daily wearer.

What use was it if she couldn't wear it whenever she wanted to?

His gaze slid to the sparkling little pile on the table and then away again. He reached for the champagne and at her nod filled her glass and then his. 'So what is it you want?'

'First, you owe your brother a new coat. You neglected to tell me it was his clothes we were burning last night.'

'Spur-of-the-moment decision. I'll buy him a new one. A better one.' Not green.

'He has a green woollen jumper. Your mother knitted it. He's very attached to it. Leave it alone.'

This time shame licked at him. 'I will.'

'Reid also wasn't impressed with your solo decision to bring a complete stranger into the home paddock, so to speak.'

'He's okay with it now, though.' Bridie gave him the look, one he'd recently interpreted to mean he needed to do more explaining. 'Bubbly, outgoing, down-to-earth girl.'

'Is that why you chose her? You've met her before?'

'Once or twice.'

'Don't make me beat more information out of you, Judah. Because I will.'

Her bluffing needed so much more work. 'She's the daughter of a guy I used to bunk with. I said I'd look her up when I got out and when I found her she was chipping cotton twelve hours a day, six days a week, doing the bookwork for a childcare centre in the evenings in exchange for childcare, and two weeks behind on her rent.'

'She has a kid?'

'A boy. He's nearly two. Last I saw, he'd fallen asleep on Reid's shoulder as Reid came out of the linen cupboard with a handful of baby blankets that used to be his.'

'Judah, Reid's a baby himself, especially in the world of relationships. What are you doing?'

'I'm bringing people into our lives because we

need help and they might need a break, and we're building things. There's another woman heading this way next week. She's a sixty-seven-year-old book-keeper I met on a ferry in Sydney, and if I don't trust my instincts now I never will. You willing to trust me, Bridie? They're both women. I wouldn't invite a man out here to stay before running it by you.'

'Then why not run the bringing of women out here past me too?'

'Because they're not as much of a threat to you? Being women and all?'

'Says who? Okay, I agree, it's unlikely they'd truss me up and stick me in a car boot, but there are other ways to pose a threat. They might not even know they're being threatening.'

'Threatening how?' He truly didn't get it.

Bridie squeezed lemon over her oysters and reached for the caviar spoon. 'You are so…so…ir-ritating! And secretive. All I'm saying is would it kill you to share your plans before they hit me and Reid like a freight train?'

'That's not *all* you're saying.' He was still try-ing to get to the bottom of that. 'I know it's going to take a while to warm up to new faces around here, but we have plans and goals that you fully support. People with specialised skills are going to be com-ing in. I'm starting with these two—three—because I figured it might ease you in gently so you *can* get used to people coming and going. I thought it would help you as well as them.'

She stared at him with stormy eyes.

'In my defence, I extended one of those offers months ago and the other one weeks ago and neither of them took me up on it at the time. I'm not hiding information from you deliberately. I'm still figuring out the decision-making process and when it's an easy one I make the call because I can.' Did he really have to remind her about the buttons?

'I'm jealous.'

'You're—' He sat back. 'Of what?'

She smiled grimly. 'Jealous of a hardworking single mum who sounds like she could use a hand and who'll have daily access to you that I don't. You met a lady in Sydney who sounds like a treasure and you never said a word. You're entitled to a life of your own and I know that. It's just… I'm coming to the conclusion that I might be a little possessive. Of you. And that's not good because you should absolutely spread yourself around, doing good things for other people. It's nice. Unlike me.' She waved towards his plate of food, and then looked down at her own plate and stabbed an oyster with her fork in a way he was pretty sure no oyster had ever been stabbed before. 'These are fresh.'

'Whoa, wait. Back up.' He kind of liked the thought of her wanting to lay claim to him. No need to beat herself up about it though. He eyed her carefully. 'Can we at least agree that I have no sexual interest in these women and that you have nothing to worry about on that front?'

'No, because then I'd have to stop arguing before I've worked my way up to making my point.'

Good old logic. Not a big player in this conversation. 'By all means make your point.'

'You seek me out, you seem to like my company, and every time I ask if you want your ring back you say *not yet*. You let me see all your eccentricities and, sod knows, they're fascinating. You're fascinating.'

He wasn't exactly sure where she was going with this but surely she would get to the reason his ring wasn't on her finger soon. 'You're not finished yet, are you?'

'No. You also consistently ignore the fact that I'm dying of lust for you.'

He hadn't touched her since returning from Sydney. He'd wanted her to know what she was getting into if she was having thoughts about being with him. He'd buried lust beneath a mountain of work and had set about showing her all the negative traits he possessed. It was important before they started anything real that she knew the real him. He cleared his throat. 'Nothing wrong with lust. Shows you didn't hate what we did last time.'

'I'd like to do it again. With you. Pretty sure I made that clear. And I get that you don't want to sully me, or overwhelm me, or whatever it is you think you're going to do, but I'm a woman of experience now—'

He snorted.

'—and I'm losing hope.'

Four little words that shattered him more effectively than a crowbar to the head.

'I can't keep giving you this much of myself if you're not interested in taking this—us—any further.'

She had a knack for honest self-reflection that terrified him. And he hadn't been giving out scraps, he'd been lowering guards so deeply nailed into his psyche that they only moved a fraction at a time. 'I'm interested.' Understatement. The thought of losing whatever it was they had made him sweat. 'At the same time, I don't want to overwhelm or disappoint you.'

'But you don't disappoint me,' she said quietly from beneath a fall of lashes. 'I want another reset of our relationship. The Conrad land is yours now. You're making waves in the business world and society thinks you're golden. There's no reason to stay engaged unless we want to. My question is: do you want to?'

'Do you?'

'You first,' she said with a smile that didn't quite meet her eyes. 'I used up all my courage putting that ring on the table.'

Was she really saying she wanted to take him on for good, flaws and all? He wasn't quite ready to admit his fierce joy at that thought, even to himself, but he wanted that ring back on her finger and, timing wise, right now wasn't nearly soon enough.

'My reputation hinges on me being a reformed

man,' he offered slowly, mind racing. 'I need to be seen as settled and steady. Combining Jeddah Creek and Devil's Kiss by way of marriage is a move my aristocratic ancestors would applaud. It's good business.'

'Not quite the reset I was imagining,' she murmured.

She deserved more, no doubt, but for all that his feelings for her ran deep—*you're in love with her,* a little voice whispered—she still figured him for a hero and he knew for a fact that he wasn't. The secret he'd held to for so many years, the one that had sent him to prison, clawed at him for release so that she could see him more fully, but he'd given his word and breaking it would have far-reaching and possibly legal consequences for all of them.

Hold your tongue. Give her what truth you can and make it enough. That was what he should be doing.

'I do want to marry you. I want that a lot, but I need you to be sure you know what you're getting into with me, and I don't think you do,' he told her baldly. 'That's my concern. You could still wear my ring while you figure it out.'

Her fingers rubbed at the spot where the ring currently wasn't. 'And would there be sex while I was figuring all this out? Because we haven't… Y'know…'

Oh, he knew. 'Again, I was giving you time to reassess.' And shore up his control. 'But if you need more to go on...'

'I do need more to go on.' They locked glances and she raised an elegant eyebrow in silent question. 'Your move.'

'Rest assured I'll be making one.'

'When?'

'Tonight.'

She changed the subject after that. Spoke about the latest set of plans for the eco cabins and how the indoor-outdoor spaces could become one with the help of sliding walls of glass that could swing out over a deck and either stay there to block the wind or slide seamlessly into the adjacent wall and disappear completely. Both the north-east and south-west walls had been tagged as slide-away. It'd be like living in a box without ends, but there were a few interior walls for privacy when needed, and a roof overhead...

The entire thing could be built in Brisbane, loaded in a container and trucked to the site and then put together in a day, by four labourers. If the cabins didn't stack up as promised, Judah figured the takeaway could be just as speedy.

The oysters were fresh and the caviar topped them off to perfection.

He helped her carry their empty plates to the kitchen once they'd devoured them. Two snappers sat ready for baking, covered in herbs and spices. 'What happens with these?'

'They're for the oven and I'm supposed to spoon the sauce over them every now and again while they're cooking. Easy as.'

She'd gone to a lot of trouble for him. 'Thank you for the wonderful meal.'

'Sometimes I want to try and impress you.'

'You always do.'

She got the food started and he wondered what she'd do if he leaned against the bench and held out his hand. Would she hesitate? Did she really understand what she would be getting into if she took him on for good?

'I have a question for you,' he began. 'It's about travel, English aristocracy and an ancestral home in the UK that needs a lot of work. On the upside, the money's now there to do all the work. If you marry me there'll be travel. Society connections to strengthen, or not, depending what kind of reception a murdering, ex-convict lord from the colonies is given.'

'Sounds horrific.'

'Yes. And you don't like to travel. I'm asking you to think hard about what marriage to me would mean. What would be required of you in order for me to fulfil my ancestral responsibilities. And I do plan to fulfil them.'

Her lips tightened. 'I'm not saying you couldn't find someone better for that role, because you definitely could. But it also sounds like someone should be there to guard your back, and who better than

some scrappy little nobody that people will under-
estimate?'

'Not for long.' At a guess.

'What would your wife even be called?'

'You'd be Lady Bridie Blake, or Lady Blake, but
it's only a prefix. A courtesy title. The barony would
pass to our firstborn son. The only courtesy titles any
of our other children could claim would be minor
ones. Reid, for example, is The Honourable Reid
Blake.'

'That's…pretty brutal on the younger kids in a
family,' she murmured. 'And women.'

'Welcome to the peerage.'

'So, uh, children. Do you want to be a father?'
she asked next.

'Yes.'

She made a small hum of approval. 'Daughters
or sons?'

'Both. It'd help if they were legitimate.'

'Well, yes. I can see that.'

He held out his hand and her smile warmed his
soul as she came to him willingly. He brushed her
hair away from her face as gently as he could, marvelling at its softness and the warmth of her skin.
'Did you just agree to marry me and have my babies?'

'Our babies,' she corrected. 'And no, I haven't
agreed to marry you yet, because you haven't asked
me yet. Not properly.'

'Marry me.' He brushed his lips against hers and

her eyes fluttered closed. An invitation to delve deeper and he took it. Salt on his tongue from the caviar, the sweetness of wine, and the innocent generosity of her every action. 'Say yes.'

She hummed in pleasure and set her hands to his waist. He could feel all his muscles clench as if he were ticklish and waiting for assault. But he wasn't ticklish, and the kisses continued. He let go of her hand and pulled her against him, soft heat to unbearable hardness.

She smiled through her kisses. 'You want me in your bed.'

'Never doubt it.'

'You can have me.'

'Still coming to terms with that. You haven't said yes to marrying me yet.'

She pulled back, out of his arms to check the food. 'You haven't said you love me yet. Or is that too much to ask?'

'It's not too much to ask.' But he still didn't know how to go about saying it.

'Let me guess,' she said drily. 'Love means making yourself vulnerable and that's hard for you.'

'Good guess.'

'Then I guess we'll just have to work on that. Can you hand me the plates from the warming oven?' she asked as she spooned sauce over steaming fish. He got her the plates, grateful for the reprieve, and she smiled her thanks. 'I hope you're hungry.'

'Famished.'

The tasty baked fish and accompanying greens, and the time it took to eat them, did nothing but ratchet up his tension. Was she going to wear his ring again or not? And how would he perform in bed? Would she want to tie him up again?

'Don't tie me up in bed this time,' he blurted, with absolutely no finesse.

She looked up from the delicate dissection of her fish. 'Okay.'

'Not that I—' He started again. 'I've been working on shoring up my self-control.'

'By yourself?' she teased.

'More or less.' She could think what she wanted and it'd probably be true. 'Those first few weeks at home… There were so many foods I hadn't tasted in years and I was a glutton for them, just shovelling it in. So many things I hadn't *done* in years and the need to do them rode me hard. And there you were. Willing.' He cleared his throat and took a sip of the very fine wine she'd served with this course. 'I had so little impulse control back then. I had freedom and no one was controlling my every move, and the curse of it all was that I could barely function. I wanted you and not in a good way. I wanted to *take*.' He shook his head. 'It wasn't right. You should have been scared of me.'

But she hadn't been.

'I have more control now. Over everything.' God, let it be true. 'Even with the occasional bonfire event.'

She lifted her glass and sipped, all effortless elegance and restraint. 'I know you do.'

'There's still a way to go.'

'I know that too.'

He refused dessert and then relented when he saw that she'd gone to the trouble of making lemon tart and had whipped cream to go with fat blackberries. They abandoned the formal dining room and Bridie served dessert on the veranda, and that, more than anything, calmed him.

He didn't know if he'd ever be much of an indoor person.

'Where do you go of a night to bed down when you don't stay here?' she asked.

'All over. Mostly the top of the escarpment if it isn't windy. River bend if I'm looking for extra shelter.'

'And you sleep in a swag?'

He nodded. Couple of rolls of latex mattress and bedclothes, all of it covered in a canvas outer and he was all set. 'Unless it's hot, and then I sleep *on* the swag in the bed of the truck.'

'What about the bugs?'

'I'm outback tough. There are no bugs.'

Bridie snorted at his utter bull.

'I wouldn't demand that of you,' he murmured, the thought of her flawless skin covered in bites not at all to his liking. 'I'm working my way in.'

'My bedroom has big screen doors out onto the

veranda. You can't see the sky from the bed, but you could be outside in an instant. I'm inviting you in.'

He set his empty bowl down and waited with gentlemanly patience while she finished the last of her lemon dessert. They still hadn't finished the wine, but he'd long since stopped drinking it and Bridie's glass was still mostly full. Nothing they decided to do next could be blamed on alcohol.

He stood and held out his hand again, and she flowed into his embrace as if she belonged there. 'Where's your bedroom?'

He followed her to it and stepped into a world of lamp-lit linen and soft-looking pillows. Jarrah floorboards grounded the room and floor rugs added touches of silver, pink and saltbush-green. The big old four-poster bed looked so inviting with its fluffy pillows and pale blue bedspread and ivory sheets. Bridie's bedroom was classy, feminine and soothing. He loved it.

'Is this all right?' she asked, and he could tell she was waiting for him to bolt.

'It's you.'

'If I do anything wrong, you'll tell me, right?'

He had to laugh. 'That's my line.'

'See, I thought your line might have been *strip*.'

Oh, hell, yes. 'Good line. Great line. Inspired. Do that.'

She made a meal out of removing her clothes. The outer layer first, and whoever had designed her lingerie needed a medal, because it made his brain shut down completely. Lace, and plenty of it, cut just so to accentuate precisely how different her body was from his. So perfect. Practically untouchable.

'Hey.' She sought and held his gaze. 'It's only me.'

So not helping.

She reached for him with greedy hands and he responded in kind. He could be needy and greedy and reverent and tender all at the same time, couldn't he? He wanted to please. Willpower was everything. It had seen him through more than seven years of hell. Surely he could appreciate those itty-bitty scraps of lace she'd worn just for him without losing his mind?

'Just touch me,' she whispered. 'I *want* your hands on me. Any argument that I'm pure and virginal is rubbish now. I'm a woman of vast experience.'

No, she was the woman he couldn't resist. Not when she gave him so much encouragement. He toppled her onto that cloud of a bed and followed her down, the soft warmth of her skin intoxicating.

'Take a chance on me,' she murmured. 'I'm right here and I want everything you're prepared to give.'

Bridie felt the tremble in his fingers and the ragged tenderness of his hands on her skin, as she in turn took her fill. She couldn't get enough of the hard muscle that defined him, or the aching tenderness of his kisses. If this was his version of ruining her, being too much for her to handle, she could almost understand his logic.

He was absolutely ruining her for all other men.

He took forever to prepare her, with his fingers and his lips, and this time when he entered her, she welcomed him with laughing enthusiasm. Her laughter seemed to set something free in him, and he smiled as he set up a rhythm that had her shooting past the Milky Way and out into orbit within minutes.

Self-consciousness never stood a chance as she rode every pulsing, ecstasy-ridden moment, and just when she thought she couldn't go again, he snaked his hand between her legs and drew one last ripple from her as he found his own release.

She needed to tell the silent Judah with the heaving chest just how good that had been. Just as soon as she regained the power of speech.

It took a few minutes, but finally she had the voice for it. 'Judah?' She snugged up into him, leaving little room for daylight, and his arms came around her, the fingers of one of his hands twining through her hair to rest at the nape of her neck.

'Mmm?'

'Let's do that again.'

CHAPTER ELEVEN

TOM STARR DEFINITELY didn't want to talk to him, thought Judah grimly, as he left yet another message for the older man to call him. The couple of times Tom *had* responded to his questions, Bridie had been her father's spokesperson.

Yes, to putting a portion of Devil's Kiss station into the conservation trust Judah had set up.

Yes, to putting the payment for the land Bridie had purchased from Judah's father into the general Devil's Kiss business account.

Judah had hoped his blunt request for permission to marry Bridie would have got Tom to pick up or at least return the call, but no.

Nothing.

That was two weeks ago.

Even Reid had tried calling. Reid had a lot of time for Tom, because of how helpful Tom had been during that four months or so Reid had been alone out here—before Judah had returned.

That man—his father's friend, the one who'd helped Reid through those toughest of times, the one who'd pulled Bridie through her almost with-drawal from society—was a man Judah didn't know.

When he thought of Tom at all it was with a mix-ture of frustration and anger, and deeply buried re-sentment that he didn't dare examine. That night... It had been two against one and Judah and Tom had been on home ground. They could have tackled Lau-rence, restrained him, neutered him on the spot... Between them they could have done *something* that didn't require ending the man. But Laurence Levit had burst from the car and charged them, and Tom, with his twenty-two-calibre shotgun that he'd used for years on the farm, hadn't hesitated and he sure as hell hadn't missed.

Judah didn't *blame* Tom for taking the shot. Not really. They'd all been running on fear and instinct.

But more and more, Judah railed against keeping secrets from Bridie. The woman who once more wore his engagement ring and who saw more of what lived inside him every day. Hopes and dreams. Struggles and failures. Hard-won success when it came to the simplest of decisions. She did more than simply en-courage him. She believed in him.

He had *Notice of Intended Marriage* paperwork burning a hole in his desk drawer, and he wanted to move on that soon. *Just do it,* he thought. *Tell her you love her and that you've never been happier and just marry her and let the past stay buried in a vow of secrecy.*

Loving her didn't have to mean confiding in her, surely.

Even if he wanted to.

These days he didn't know what exactly it was that shook him from her bed in the dark hours of most mornings, but he tried to make it up to her. He'd taken to collecting wildflowers and greenery, whatever he could find, and returning with a fistful and either leaving them on her doorstep or bringing them with him to breakfast.

Bridie had clear run out of vases but her eyes would still light up every time he handed her a posy.

'Heard anything from your father?' he asked one morning after a night that had made him forget his own name and a morning spent watching the sun rise from the top of Devil's Peak. He was back on her veranda now with a coffee in hand, no sugar, and way too much cream.

'Yes.' Bridie sat in an old rocking chair wearing a stripy pink T-shirt and darker pink bed shorts, her hair in a messy bun and breakfast in hand; to Judah she'd never looked more beautiful. 'He bought an opal mine in Lightning Ridge, complete with underground home and a hole-in-the-wall shop front, and apparently he *does* mean hole in the wall. I don't know what's going on with him. He's too old to be having a midlife crisis and he hasn't said anything about meeting a woman, but what other reasons are there for his refusal to come home? He has no interest in the management of Devil's Kiss any more and I truly don't understand. This is his home. Why won't he come *home*?'

So Judah rang again, and this time Tom picked up.

'You're a hard man to reach.' Judah spoke first.

'And you're relentless,' grumbled the older man.

'Bridie's worried about you.'

''M fine.'

'Reid misses you too.' Might as well turn those screws.

'They have you now.'

Definitely not the answer he'd been expecting. 'You have a problem with me.' Statement, not question. 'Why? I've kept every promise I've ever made. Especially to you.'

'What do you want?' He could barely hear the older man.

'Permission to marry your daughter.'

'You don't need it.'

That wasn't the point. 'It's customary to ask for it.'

The other man said nothing.

Judah gritted his teeth before he spoke again. Bridie loved this man. Reid thought the world of him. 'You left. The minute I got home you left and I don't understand why. You have people here who love you and people contemplating big changes in their lives, and you're not here for them. Why not? What have I done wrong?'

'Nothing,' Tom rasped after long moments. 'But every time I look at you I feel ashamed at what I've put you through. The trial. Your sentence. The impact it had on your parents and your brother. On you. I'd go back in time and do things differently if I could, but I can't, and it pains me. It pains me to look at you and know in my heart what your generosity has cost you. I don't know how to make it up to you. So I try not to look at you at all.'

'Come home.' Judah didn't want Tom Starr exiled from the life he'd once loved. 'Take a look at what we're building here. Be a part of it again. And if your conscience is troubling you, we can sit down together, with Bridie, and tell her what really happened that night.'

Silence.

'Is that a no?'

'Why?' He could barely hear the other man. 'Why on earth would you want to do that?'

'Did *you* keep secrets from *your* wife?' Judah snapped, losing what little patience he had left. 'I don't *want* to marry your daughter and have to lie to her about that night for the rest of our lives,' he said, abandoning all pretence that he gave a damn about Tomas's conscience. He wanted his own conscience clear. He wanted Bridie to know what she was getting when she chose him. 'Is that really too much to ask?'

He blundered on. 'What if we sat her down and explained everything and that we did what we did to protect her? Surely she'd understand.' And be okay with a father who'd killed to protect her and a future husband who hadn't, but at least there'd be no more lies.

Tom Starr didn't reply.

'Can you at least think about it?'

'You gave me your word.'

'I know. And I've never broken it, even though you broke yours when you told my father what you did. But you could release me from my vow.' He couldn't see the other man to read his face. He had no idea what Tom Starr was thinking. There was just this sea of silence.

'We need to think about this.' There was a world of weariness in the older man's voice. 'If word ever got out I could go to prison. You could go *back* to prison. Is that what you want?'

'Word wouldn't get out because Bridie wouldn't tell anyone.'

'Are you sure about that? Because I'm not. Do you really think we should burden her with a secret she can never share without her whole world crumbling? *And* we'd be making her an accessory after the fact. Is telling her the truth really worth all that?'

The older man was right. He was being a fool. A romantic, idiotic fool. 'You're right.'

'I'm sorry, son, but I just don't see the sense in telling Bridie what happened that night and dragging her into the pit with us. You promised to protect her.'

'I know.'

'You gave me your word.'

'I'll keep it.'

'I know you will.' There was an ache in the older man's voice that he didn't know what to do with. An ache in his own heart because there was no way around this. Tom Starr was right and that was the end of it.

Their secret had to be kept.

Gert was baking and Bridie was stacking groceries; music was blaring and the sun had yet to sap the will to move. All in all, Bridie decided, life was good and she'd never deny it.

'Have you met the new people over at Jeddah Creek yet?' asked Gert.

'Yep.' A couple of times over, plenty long enough to form some opinions. 'Mary the bookkeeper is a sweetheart, but she's kind of shocked by outback living. I don't know if she'll stay.'

'What about the young one?'

'Kaylee? She's a hoot. Big laugh, can-do attitude, tough as nails. And grateful, y'know? In that way that says she's seen a lot of rough road in her life. I have a feeling she'll stay—at least for a while. Her little guy's not even two yet. Cute kid. Judah and Reid are so protective of him. You should see them.'

Gert snorted. 'Sounds about right. They have that ruling class serve-and-protect mentality, same as their grandfather did. And their father did too, before his liking for a drink ruined him.'

'Yeah, maybe.' Bridie didn't know what bits of

Gert's conversation she was agreeing with, but it probably didn't matter.

'You expecting visitors?' Gert asked next.

'Nope.'

'Because there's a line of dust heading in from the east and it's just turned into your driveway.'

The driveway was two kilometres long. Plenty of time for her and Gert to head on out to the veranda and wait. Eventually Bridie got a good enough look at the vehicle to figure out who it was. 'It's my father.'

'Huh,' huffed Gert and headed back inside. Bridie waited, and when her father pulled up and stepped from the cab, she unfolded her crossed arms and ran to greet him. His hug was as solidly comforting as it had always been. 'Hello, stranger.'

'Daughter.' He pulled back. 'You're looking bright.'

'It's all this newfound independence,' she countered drily. 'I've missed you, though.'

He looked uncomfortable. 'I needed to do a bit of thinking.'

'Finished yet?'

'Doubtful. Your aunt sent a present along for you. It's in the back.'

'You saw her? Is she well?'

He nodded. 'Got herself a good man who thinks the world of her.' His gaze didn't stray from Bridie's face. 'I hear you have one of those too.'

They headed into the kitchen, where Gert had

coffee on and ginger nuts in the oven. Her father smiled. Gert didn't.

'Tomas Starr, is that you? I barely remember what you look like.'

'And a good day to you too, Gert.'

The older woman fixed him with a gimlet glare. 'Your room's not made up.'

'I can make a bed,' her father said easily.

'Are you back to stay?' Bridie asked, interrupting before war broke out.

Her father shrugged. 'For a while. Mainly to see if you need anything and whether all the changes are working out.'

'They are.' She'd missed having him around. She wanted him back and for more than just a while. 'Opal miner now, huh? I would never have guessed.'

He dug in his pocket and pulled out two good-sized stones and handed one to her and one to Gert. 'It's a bit of fun.'

'Black opal.' Gert held hers up to the light. 'Tom Starr, you canny ass.'

'Plenty more where that came from,' he offered. 'You're both welcome to join me next time I head down that way.'

'Do I get to keep this opal?' asked Gert.

'Yes, it's for you. Thanks for keeping an eye on Bridie while I was gone.'

'Next time you take off for parts unknown, check in more,' Gert scolded. 'Your daughter worries about you. Those Blake boys have been worried about you too, especially Reid. He looks up to you. You encouraged that and now you've let him down.'

'He has Judah now,' her father countered.

Gert glared at him. 'And you don't think Judah could have used your support too? Tomas Starr, I never took you for such a fool.'

'Live and learn, Gert,' her father said quietly as he hooked his leg around a kitchen stool and took a seat. 'Live and learn.'

Gert headed off to the Blakes' at noon—nothing disrupted her schedule if she could help it, not even the return of the prodigal father. Bridie welcomed the privacy; she had so much to tell her father, from the success of her exhibitions to the photography job she'd agreed to in South Australia that meant she'd be away for a week, staying on a property that had a huge woolshed with a heritage and history she found fascinating. She wanted to tell him she'd sold the season's steers for an excellent price, but had resisted culling any of the main herd when buyers had asked for more meat of any kind. The Devil's Kiss stockmen would have known which animals to cull, no question, but it was traditionally her father's role and she hadn't wanted to overstep.

She waited until after dinner when their bellies were full of home-grown steak, jacket potatoes, asparagus and sweetcorn, and her father had settled into his favourite rocking chair on the veranda, before she broached more personal topics.

'Judah's been trying to reach you.'

'He did.' Her father's eyes were darkly shadowed. 'He asked me for your hand in marriage. He's old-fashioned that way.'

'Did you give him your blessing?'

'We talked.'

Bridie's blood ran cold. Never in a million years had she thought her father would hold Judah's past against him. 'He's a good man, Dad. The best. And I am so...so in love with him.'

'He puts me to shame.' Her father looked away, out over the home paddock and on to the horizon. He took a deep breath. 'What do you remember about the night that bastard took you?'

She shook her head. She hated remembering any of it. 'Laurence came to the door and I let him in. Offered him a coffee. He'd come all this way to clear the air between us, he said, and no one else was here.'

'After that,' her father ordered gruffly.

'I told him I wasn't going back to modelling. It wasn't what he wanted to hear. He grabbed me. I struggled. He hit me. I passed out. I remember coming to, bound and gagged in the boot of a car. I remember you and Judah rescuing me and Levit bleeding out in the dirt.'

Her father nodded. 'And on the surface that's exactly what happened. Never forget, Bridie girl, that I love you. That I did everything in my power to protect you. And that Judah went way beyond what could be expected of any man to protect you too.'

'I know this already.'

But her father shook his head, leaned forward and brought the rocker to a halt. He stared at the weathered wooden floorboards as if they were the most fascinating things he'd ever seen. 'No, you don't. Not everything. We kept something from you.'

'What do you mean?'

'Judah didn't kill the bastard who kidnapped you, Bridie. I did.'

Don't do anything rash. Bridie used the words as a mantra during her drive to Jeddah Creek homestead. Don't act out. *Listen* to what Judah had to say. And all the while, with every red dust kilometre, the foundations of her world crumbled. Her father was a killer and a liar who'd sold his soul to protect her. And Judah…not a killer, but still a liar who'd paid a huge price for his deception. How could he have chosen to do that for her and her father? She didn't understand.

Bridie checked her speed as she approached the main house. There was a child living in the shearer's quarters these days and other new people about and it wouldn't do to run over them. She parked next to Gert's truck and took the stairs two at a time, only to almost bump into Reid, who looked to be on his way out.

'Whoa, steady Freddie.' He sidestepped her just in time.

'Judah around?'

'In his office.' Judah had turned the sitting room next to the library into his office. It had French doors leading onto the veranda and Bridie didn't bother going through the house to get there.

Judah looked up from his seat behind the desk as she entered, a smile crinkling his eyes. 'Just in time,' he said. 'The cabin plans are in.'

But she didn't want to pour over building plans with him. 'I've just been speaking with my father.'

'Gert said he was back.' He lifted an eyebrow. 'Bearing opals.'

Bridie didn't want to talk about little coloured stones. 'He said you'd asked for his permission to marry me.'

'I did.'

Judah sat back in his chair, everything about him easy and welcoming, except for those watchful, wary eyes.

'You want to know what else he told me?' She couldn't keep the rage out of her voice and it seemed useless to even try.

'That he refused to give it?'

She hadn't known *that*. Apparently she didn't know a lot of things that happened around here. 'He told me what happened that night, Judah. What really happened.'

She'd never seen a person shut down so fast. Any openness in his beautiful strong face disappeared like spilt water in a sandy desert. 'What do you mean?'

'What do you *think* I mean?' she cried. 'Did my father kill Laurence Levit, or did you? Because my father just told me he did it!'

Not by a blink did Judah betray any discomfort. 'I've said all I'm ever going to say about that. I was convicted and I've done my time. Move on.'

'But my father—'

'Is mistaken.'

'Well, one of you is lying! And I'm inclined to believe him.'

Judah shrugged.

'Judah, please. *Talk* to me.'

'And accomplish what? Shall I make you complicit in a possible cover-up that took place years ago? Should I break the oath I might have made to your father to take the details of that night to my grave? What if I didn't shoot Levit? Do you want to see me up on perjury charges and your father locked up? Is that it?'

'No, I—'

'Then *stop* asking questions. Your father is a deluded old man. Don't believe him.'

But she did believe her father's startling words. That was the problem. 'But why would you *do* such a thing? Why would a young man with *everything* going for him—money, status, a loving family, good looks and good health—why would he choose to be locked up for something he didn't do? Will you at least offer me a theoretical answer to that question?' If Judah wasn't going to confirm a damn thing, could they at least play pretend while she got to the bottom of everyone's actions? 'Can't you open up to me just a little?' she pleaded. 'Because I don't understand. I just don't get it.'

'Is he of the ruling class?' Judah steepled his fingers and held her gaze, looking every inch the aristocrat. 'Or, y'know what? Scrap that. Maybe he'd simply been raised to serve and protect those in his care—the old, the frail, the *children*.'

'But if my father was the one who took the shot, why didn't he say so at the time? They might have gone easy on him. Easier than they went on you.'

'And who would have taken you in? Who would have cared for you the way your father did? Who would have had the love and the patience to help put you back together again? Your aunt? She was already struggling with her own issues. You don't have any other family. Your father was it. Who better to love and protect you than him? What if your father and that foolish young man made a split-second decision to protect you? And then did so.'

She had no answer for him. 'I'm not a child any more.'

'I know that.'

'You can tell me the truth.'

'Good, then hear this.' He spread his hands. 'I love you. And I'll protect you with my last breath, don't ever doubt it. This is me protecting you.'

Not exactly how she'd imagined his first declaration of love for her would go.

He watched as she twisted her engagement ring around and around. 'Are you going to keep that on?'

She didn't know. She was so *angry* with him. For stepping up to take the blame for something he didn't do. For defending his action as the right thing to do, never mind what it had cost him. For protecting her still. 'I'm so sorry,' she whispered.

'You're not to blame. You owe me nothing. And if you're going to take that ring off, *for God's sake just do it*!' He looked more rattled than she'd ever seen him, and she'd seen him rattled a lot. He ran an unsteady hand through his hair. 'I can't stand to watch you playing with it. That's my heart you're holding in your hands.'

His outburst jolted her some way towards recognising how hard this conversation must be for him too. 'You have to stop protecting me,' she defended weakly, even as she clasped her hands behind her back. No fiddling with the ring. Just a vicelike grip of one hand over the tennis bracelet on her wrist.

He glared at her with stormy eyes. 'I will *never* not protect you.'

'Truth is important,' she said next. 'Especially in a marriage.'

'How important?' His gaze didn't leave hers. 'If your father says he pulled that trigger I'll call him a crazy old coot and a liar to his face. If I'm not measuring up to some ideal you have in your head about what you want in a man and truth in marriage, walk away. Run. Because this is who I am.'

'I—' If she believed her father—and she did—she also had to believe that the two most important people in her life had been lying to her all along. Judah was *still* lying to her. 'I'm so confused.'

'It's really pretty simple from where I'm standing. You either understand where I'm coming from or you don't.'

She was confused and shattered. Judah was lying about who pulled that trigger. She knew he was lying. He *knew* she knew he was lying. But he wouldn't stop. 'I need time. I don't know what to think.'

He rose from his chair and headed for the interior door that led to a hallway inside the house. 'Let me know what you decide.'

'Wait!'

He stopped.

'You said you love me.' She hadn't imagined that, had she?

'I do.' He started walking towards the door again. 'It doesn't mean you have to love me back. That's not how it works.'

Moments later he was gone.

CHAPTER TWELVE

BRIDIE DROVE HOME, half expecting her father to have taken off again, but he met her at the door, no questions on his tongue but his eyes awhirl with them. She didn't know what to say to him, she really didn't.

'Judah says you're a lying old coot,' she offered finally. Might as well start at the top. 'So let's make ourselves a cup of tea and figure out where to go from here.'

She let the motions soothe her as she filled the teapot with leaves from the little tin canister that had sat on the kitchen shelf forever. Her father took his black and strong. She took hers with milk and liked it weaker, so she made sure she took first pour. And all the time she marshalled her thoughts and arguments so that the two most important people in her life would remain in her life. 'Let's take it out to the veranda.'

He picked up his cup and she followed him out, unsurprised when he chose the northern veranda with its relentlessly bright light that reached deep into the veranda and sometimes hit the windows. It had the best views, unmarred by garden trees. It was red dirt and spinifex as far as the eye could see, with very little variation in topography. Their most brutal view, in many ways. There wasn't a scrap of civilisation in it.

She sat down beside him on the veranda ledge and nudged his shoulder with hers. They both sipped deeply of the tea.

'I've missed this,' he murmured.

'You didn't have to leave.'

'Needed to get my head on straight,' he said, and she thought about that. About what Judah's return might have done to him. Judah could reject the notion all he liked but he'd done so much for them. So much more than anyone could have asked of him. And all Judah had asked of them was to let it go and move forward.

'Thing is,' she continued doggedly, 'me, you, Aunt Beth—we can all blame ourselves for the decisions that led us to that moment.' She took her father's calloused hand, with the knuckles just starting to thicken with arthritis, and held on tight. 'I should never have chosen modelling and brought Laurence Levit into our lives. Aunt Beth should have known better than to be taken in by him, but she had barely more experience with predatory men than I did. You could have come to Paris with us and pegged him as a bad one or maybe you wouldn't have, who knows? Point is, he got hold of us and then kept on coming. The law didn't stop him. Those AVOs we had out against him meant nothing out here. Can we agree on that? That Laurence Levit wasn't stopped by ordinary means?'

Her father's hand tightened around hers, a squeeze to show he was listening. 'We can.'

'So whatever happened, happened. And one way or another we owe Judah more than we can ever say. Can we agree on that too?'

'Yes.'

She took a deep breath and exhaled noisily. 'The only payment Judah wants is for us to look forward rather than back, and I am on board with that. I can understand you not being in the same place, and that feelings of guilt or shame or the need for penance might be eating at you, but I want you to know that in my eyes you are both heroes. Laurence crossed a line when he took me. All the character witnesses they put on the stand, all those people who said he was an upstanding man, they didn't look into his eyes and see their own death staring back at them. I did, and it was me or him, Dad. Me or him. I'm glad you chose me.'

Her father squeezed her hand and then carefully let it go, but Bridie wasn't finished yet.

'Judah's adamant he did the deed and he knows I don't believe him, but he won't tell the truth. He's protecting us. Even if I'd rather he didn't this time around.'

'He's a man of his word,' her father muttered with far more complacency than Bridie thought was warranted. 'But look on the bright side, at least now you know the truth, even if he never confirms it. No more secrets between you two. A clean slate before marriage. That's a good thing, so I'm told.'

Wait. 'Did you know Judah was never going to rat you out?'

Her father shrugged. 'Might've.'

Holy—

'That's…' She had no words.

'Inspired?'

More like brutally self-serving. 'You left him to hang. Again.'

'I knew he loved you and wanted to marry you. I knew he could never tell you what really happened, no matter how much he wanted to. Not if he wanted to protect you from knowing too much. But if *I* told you, he could still deny it and we'd all be protected. And you'd know what he wanted you to know but could never tell you.'

'That's insane.'

'It worked.'

Heaven help her it had, but not without cost. She remembered Judah's stricken face and furious outburst when she'd been twisting her engagement ring around and around. When she'd been doing her damnedest to understand his position. 'You took a huge risk, playing us like that.'

'It worked.' He looked towards the horizon. To the harsh land that set a person against relying on others to fix their problems. 'No secrets between you now. Be happy. Reach out for all the happiness you can hold and never take it for granted.'

'Promise me you'll stay a part of our lives,' she pressed.

Her father offered up the ghost of a smile. 'I've got opal seams to find.'

'Then promise me you'll visit often and remember on a daily basis how much I love you and want you in my life.'

'Judah might prefer otherwise. What did he call me? A lying old coot?'

'Well, you are,' she felt compelled to point out. He was also her father. The same father who'd given her the time and space in which to heal from her ordeal. The one who'd helped her live her best life.

Bridie leaned her head against the veranda post. 'I didn't handle my confrontation with Judah very well. I got all caught up in truth-telling and couldn't see the bigger picture.' *Breathe in, breathe out and try not to panic.* 'It's possible he thinks I'm going to dump him.'

Her father lowered his cup. 'Are you?'

'No.' A world of no. 'I'm going to marry him and protect him and cherish him as best I can, and he's never going to think I don't love him for being the man he is. Not for a second. Not even a fraction of a second.'

'Best get on that.'

'I will.'

Bridie had a plan. Granted, it would take the assistance of several other people in order for her to pull it off, but the end result was going to show Judah exactly how much she cherished him and all that he was.

Her first call was to Reid, and he offered no quarter, speaking before she'd even said a word. 'What have you done to my brother? He's been working like a demon all morning to distract himself from thinking your engagement is off.'

'It's not off.'

'Mind telling him that? In person? Soon? As in, I will come and get you in the helicopter right now.'

'That's the spirit.' Might as well go with the flow. 'Tell him I love him like crazy and that the engagement is very much on. Tell him that I'm putting together an apology surprise for him and that you'll pick him up an hour before sunset for a helicopter joyride with me at the end of it. That's all you need to say. Can you do that?'

'Better coming from you.'

'Apart from that, which I will see to, trust me, I need your helicopter and your services as a pilot for the rest of the day. I'll pay triple the going rate. And sheets. I need every sheet you've got that's not already on a bed.'

'Sheets,' he echoed doubtfully.

'For when I run out of rocks and fallen branches. Oh, and do you have any toilet paper?'

'No way am I giving up my share of the toilet paper. You've gotta be family for that.'

'Bring it anyway,' she urged.

'You're sounding a little bit mad today. Are you

aware of this?' He really was a sweet and mostly biddable man.

'I am mad. I'm mad at myself for letting your brother doubt his worth for a second.'

'I'm going to put you on speaker phone now because Judah's just walked in, and you're going to put him out of his misery by telling him that.'

'Wait! Will you help me? It'll be worth it, I promise. I'm aiming to create a truly memorable moment.'

'Speaker phone. Now.'

'Wait!' But she didn't think Reid had been open to influence on this particular issue. 'Judah?'

'Bridie,' he replied evenly.

Right, so…speakerphone. 'I'm, uh, hi!' So not ready to confront him yet.

Silence.

Bridie closed her eyes, took a deep breath and began. 'So, yesterday was tough to navigate. Lots of new and surprising information to think about, you know?' She rushed on without waiting for more astonishingly loud silence. 'But I don't want to call off our engagement. You are without question the finest man I know. I want to marry you, cheer for you, laugh with you and cherish all the little pieces that make you who you are. I still want that for us.'

No one spoke.

Bridie cringed, wishing she could see how her words were being received. 'Do you—is that what you want?'

She heard a heavy sigh, but wasn't sure whose it was. 'Did someone just huff?'

'That was me,' confessed Reid. 'I'm trying to get my white-knuckled, tongue-tied brother to say something at this very special moment in time but he's not responding to my cues.'

And then Judah spoke. 'Bridie, you don't have to do this. You don't owe me a damn thing.'

'Wait!' yelped Reid. 'What?' There was the sound of a scuffle and muffled words she couldn't quite hear and then Reid in her ear again. 'Sorry I interrupted. My brother hasn't quite finished speaking yet.'

She waited. And waited.

And held her breath and *waited*.

'I'm yours.' Rough-cut words that sounded as if Judah had carved them out of his heart just for her. 'Yes, that's what I want. So much.'

'Great. That's perfect. *You're* perfect.' Even if he wasn't one for fancy words. She could be the fancy-word provider. Not a problem. 'Will you join me for an hour before sunset? And probably after the sun sets too? I want to spoil you to make up for my... confusion...yesterday.'

'No need,' Judah rumbled. 'It's forgotten.'

'No, it's not, even though we'll never mention it again. Will you please let Reid bring you to me this afternoon, no questions asked?'

'Yes.'

Yes! She punched the air with her fist. 'See you then. Oh, and, Reid?'

'My rotor blades are at your service, future favourite sister-in-law.'

'I'm really glad I get a little brother out of this deal too.' And not just because she really needed his help if she had any hope of pulling her rapidly forming plans together in a day. 'How soon can you get here? I have so much for you to do.'

Reid found Judah in his office shortly after five that afternoon. Judah studied his brother, looking for clues as to what he'd been up to, but Reid's aviator sunglasses hid his eyes and nothing else about him looked any different than it had this morning. Well-worn jeans, loose T-shirt, work boots, ready grin. Reid had been back twice throughout the afternoon to refuel, so he'd sure as hell been covering some ground in his compact two-seater helicopter.

'Ready to go find your intended?'

Reid had taken to all but bouncing up and down on the balls of his feet. Nervous energy was a new look for Reid and instantly made Judah even more suspicious about what the afternoon held in store. 'Am I going to like this surprise?'

'God, I hope so,' muttered Reid. 'If you don't, I'm thinking of relocating to Canada for a recovery holiday. Got your wallet?'

'What for?' Who needed a wallet around here?

'ID in case we crash. I've been reading up on my aviation rules.'

His brother's words were almost believable. Only not.

'Just bring your wallet.' Reid spread his arms out

imploringly. One of his forearms had an ugly red scrape on it that Judah was pretty sure hadn't been there this morning. 'C'mon, I've been humouring Bridie all afternoon and it was a very tough gig. Is it too much to ask that you take your wallet out of your desk drawer and shove it in your back pocket?'

'Testy.' But he did as his brother asked, and Reid's smile reappeared.

'How about a shirt with a collar?' Reid suggested next and Judah eyed him narrowly.

'Why?'

'Have I mentioned the amount of *effort* I've expended this afternoon on your behalf? Not to mention the effort Bridie's put in. Last I saw her she was absolutely filthy, headed for a shower and obsessing about whether she had anything suitable to wear. Silk was mentioned, along with whether she had time to wash and dry her hair and do anything with it. I have never run away faster, but out of the goodness of my very kind heart I'm sharing this information with you in case you want to go and change your shirt.'

So Judah went to the adjacent walk-in cupboard and changed his shirt. 'Anything else?'

'Decent boots. Not work boots.'

'Is this a formal dinner situation?' Because he'd been expecting something a little more casual. Picnic from the back of her Land Rover somewhere out on the plains while the sun went down.

'I am sworn to secrecy. But if we don't get cracking we're going to be late. Sunset waits for no man.'

It wasn't until they were walking to the helicopter that Judah spoke again. 'Where are we going?'

'Up.'

'Can you be any more specific?'

'Nope.'

Reid flew helicopters with the confidence only youth and long hours in the seat could bring. Mustering would see them flying low and darting about, but this time he took them high and smooth and put them on a north-east course towards river bend. Not so far to go, then, and he wondered why Bridie hadn't simply asked him to drive there. But Reid overshot the mark, so maybe river bend wasn't their destination at all. Reid then confused him twice over by swinging them around to approach the river again, this time with the sun behind them.

And then he saw it: a word spelled out on the ground with a combination of rocks, dead branches and some kind of white material.

The word was STRENGTH.

'I'm working from a script here, so let me get it right,' Reid told him through their headset two-ways. 'This is what Bridie sees in you. A man of strength. I see it too.'

Before Judah could comment, Reid swung the helicopter around in a show-off move and headed west.

Another word waited for them in the channel country, and it was as if a demented fairy had scoured the land for as many moveable rocks as they could find.

COURAGE was the word.

'This too,' said Reid, and circled it twice before taking them north.

'There's more?'

'Better believe it. Which is the point of this whole exercise. That you come to believe what she sees in you. Good thing she ran out of fabric.'

The next word said HONOUR.

'I like that one for you,' said Reid. 'I think it's my favourite.'

The next word was RESILIENCE, and it had been shaped out of some kind of heavy-duty canvas, pinned down by tent pegs and rocks.

'That one nearly did her in,' said tour guide Reid, while Judah sat there awash in words and none of them his. 'I had to help her with it because she was nowhere near done when I came to pick her up. Too many letters, man, way too many letters and not enough rocks in the world. Try PEP, I said. What about GRIT? I didn't do badly in my English exams, I had suggestions, but no. It had to be RESILIENCE. There's not a scrap of tarpaulin left in her shed.' Reid paused. 'Or ours.'

The next word was HOPE.

'She says a man without hope can't begin to imagine the future the way you do. Or work so hard to make it happen the way you do. Can't say I disagree with her. She had more words—it was a very long list, but there's only one more.'

'Good.' Because they were doing him in.

The last word was JOY.

'Joy?' he asked gruffly. 'Me? Now I'm sure she needs glasses.'

'Yeah.' Reid laughed. 'I queried that one too, but she swears there's a lifetime of it in store for you if you'll take her on. I'm to give you this now.' Reid handed him a white envelope. 'To read.'

In the envelope was a sheet of office paperwork, and words printed in a fancy font inviting him to the wedding of Miss Bridie Elizabeth Starr and Lord Judah Leopold Blake.

Date: Today
Time: Sunset
RSVP: Landing means I Do

'I'm your best man if that's what you want,' said Reid. 'And there's a wedding party waiting for you just over those trees. Gert is matron of honour and Tomas is the FOB—that's father of the bride—and he'll be giving Bridie away. I am bang up on wedding abbreviations after today. Old Ernie reckons he can legitimately marry you as long as you have some ID. I think he's dreaming, but what do I know?'

'Take us down.'

But Reid didn't take them down. Instead he flew over the clump of trees to reveal a pathway of rocks that led to a small group of people. Bridie stood out like a beacon in a slim white gown with tiny shoulder straps and the rest of it pretty much fell straight to the ground. Her riot of hair had been pulled away from her face and styled instead to cascade down her back. She held a posy stuffed haphazardly with desert flowers, the kind he'd taken to finding for her after a night beneath the stars.

'Reid. *Take us down.*'

'Those are the words I wanted to hear. Right after *Yes, oh, wise, hardworking and patient brother, I want you to be my best man.*'

'I want you to be my best man.'

'What happened to wise, hardworking and patient? You can't hog *all* the good words.'

'Reid, that woman down there is my North Star, my refuge and my soul. Get me down there before she changes her mind.'

'They're landing,' said Gert, and Bridie's heart soared.

Proving her love for Judah by springing a surprise wedding on him had seemed like a good idea at the time, but as everything came together, with Reid dropping her back at the homestead before flitting off to collect Gert, and then Ernie, and finally Judah, second thoughts had taken hold. What if Judah didn't want to marry her yet? What if he did want to marry her but wanted a different kind of wedding altogether? One that took a year or two to plan and involved many aristocratic guests? Maybe his inherited title meant he had to follow lots of rules before it was official?

Not that he was necessarily one for rules. He had

his own unwavering code of honour and she loved him all the more for it.

She took a deep breath. In, out. In, out. While a brilliant afternoon sun gently kissed the horizon.

'It's normal to be a little bit nervous,' said Gert. 'And usually, it's the man standing here waiting for his bride.'

'Yay for equality,' offered Bridie weakly. She hadn't really thought this part of the afternoon through. Standing there scouring the sky and waiting for him to show had been *excruciating*.

She took a deep breath and exhaled noisily. She *had* given him the chance to simply fly away. Give him the invitation when you're on the last word, she'd told Reid. And then take him wherever he wants to go.

She'd had no plan B for if he didn't arrive, other than painfully, publicly falling to pieces. Why was it taking Reid so damn long to land the helicopter?

'Turn around and let me fuss over you,' said Gert, taking charge. The older woman's concerned blue gaze met hers as she tucked a strand of Bridie's hair behind her ear. 'You look so beautiful. So very ready to make that man happy, and there's no one who deserves happiness more than him.'

'I know.' She blew out another breath. Heaven knew what she'd be like in childbirth. Probably hyperventilating all over the place. 'I've got this.' She took Gert's hand and placed it over her racing heart. 'See?'

'Relax, child. He's here.'

She was never not going to associate the sound of the helicopter powering down with this moment. 'Is he heading our way?'

The older woman nodded and squeezed Bridie's hand before letting go. 'Tomas, you stand over here next to Ernie and I'll stand here, and all Judah and Reid have to do when they get here is step into place.'

Which they did.

Judah turned towards her, outback strong in dusty boots, well-worn jeans, collared shirt with the sleeves rolled up and eyes that searched her face. 'Hey.'

'Hey.' Forget butterflies in her stomach. She croaked like a frog.

'Beautiful sunset,' he said next, and Reid elbowed him in the ribs.

'North Star,' Reid muttered around a fit of totally fake coughing.

Judah jostled him back, his gaze not leaving her face. 'And still nowhere near as incredible as you,' he added quietly. 'Are you ready to take on the world with me?'

'I'm ready.' So very ready to love this man for ever.

So Ernie married them.

EPILOGUE

Judah watched from his vantage point at one end of the ground-floor veranda as his guests spilled out of the crowded ballroom and into the night. Jeddah Creek station glowed with the care that only endless money and strong vision could bring. Planes were parked wing to wing in the outer home paddock and tents had sprung up beside the planes that didn't have sleeping quarters built in. Last year's welcome home ball had only whetted people's appetite for another taste of Judah Blake, philanthropist, and the vast land protection initiatives he spearheaded.

A warm and playful breeze whipped at the wraps and the hair of the ladies present and the stars in the sky that he never took for granted drew gasps from the city folk not used to such a generous display.

This past year had been a rewarding one. Almost as if every mad idea for a better future he'd ever had in the past nine years was being acted out in front of him. Money, so much money available for his projects. Remote area cabins that were architectural marvels. Scientific research projects. Channel country preservation. His brilliant, talented, beautiful wife…

Bridie was inside the ballroom somewhere, but chances were she'd find him soon enough. She still wasn't one for big crowds, and her growing status as an artist made her nervous at times, but she was his fiercest defender and she was in there tonight talking paint colours with his godmother, Eleanor. Bridie wasn't just his North Star. She was all the stars in the sky.

He checked his clothes. White shirt cuffs with a quarter inch showing below the sleeve of his suit. His father's watch, and his grandfather's before that, partly visible when he extended his hand. Such things mattered to some of the people he was courting here tonight.

Bridie wore a pale blue gown tonight, her shoulders bare, a fitted bodice and a sleek fall of silk starting somewhere around her waist and finishing at the floor. A stunning blue opal, outlined in silver filigree, hung from a ribbon around her neck, her father's work. Bridie had already fielded a number of questions about the piece and had gleefully turned them towards her father, especially the single ladies of good nature and mature age. Tomas, who epitomised the rugged, wary outback loner, had suffered the first few ladies with dogged, near-mute politeness, which only seemed to make the ladies try even harder to put him at ease.

Tomas had last been seen fleeing from the ballroom, with Bridie's delighted laughter lingering in his wake.

Bridie laughed a lot these days and Judah never tired of the sound.

And then there was her beauty. Call him biased, but these days her considerable physical beauty seemed somehow lit from within. Contentment, she called it. *Or maybe it's wonder,* she'd once said to him. So many new experiences had come her way this past year and she seemed determined to approach every one of them with wonder and gratitude.

Approaches like that were contagious, no question, given that he'd recently started doing the same.

It was all too easy to be grateful for the life he was living now.

'Your wife has requested your presence at her side,' said Reid, sliding into place beside him. Reid was a hair taller than Judah these days and broader across the shoulders. Responsibility sat more easily on those shoulders, and with it came an easy confidence his brother had more than earned.

If Judah was the visionary and dealmaker of the trio, then Reid was the project manager with the people skills to make it happen. Bridie was their media manager with full control over visual promotional material and how and where it was displayed.

Sometimes, when he was feeling especially smug, Judah thought that together the three of them could change the world.

'She still with Lady Eleanor?'

Reid nodded.

'Have you persuaded your school friend to come and chef for us yet?'

'He says he can give us six months. I'm holding out for twelve so that he's here when the visiting astrophysicists arrive. Have you seen their list of dietary requirements? Talk about special.'

'Double what you're offering him.'

'I love spending your money. Consider it done.' Reid smiled cheerfully. 'Shouldn't you be on your way to rescue your North Star, your refuge and your soul?'

He was never going to live that down.

He was, however, moving towards the ballroom door.

He found her to one side of the dance floor, his godmother nowhere in sight. She watched him walk towards her with a smile she just didn't give anyone else. He tried to figure out what was different about the ones she saved for him but so far he hadn't been able to.

Hooked him every time.

'Dance with me,' he said when he reached her and held out his hand, and she slid hers into it, warm and utterly sure of her welcome.

And why wouldn't she be? She had him wrapped around her little finger.

'I'd like the photographer here tonight to take some photos of us dancing,' she said. 'That okay by you?'

'What for?'

'Private use only. You, me, the family photo album. They'd come after the brilliant ones of our first kiss and the blurry ones Reid took of our wedding.'

She'd kept her promise about always asking before taking pictures of him. He'd never quite got over how exposed he'd felt when looking at a picture of himself, never mind that he carried one small, well-creased picture of them kissing in the rain in his wallet. Every time he looked at it, he was transported back to the purest moment of freedom he'd ever felt.

He also knew how much Bridie regretted not having a single decent photo of their wedding. Didn't matter to him so much.

He'd memorised every moment. 'Okay.'

She nodded and sent a thumbs up to someone off to the side, presumably the photographer, and then he turned her in his arms and put a hand to the back of her waist.

They still hadn't learned how to dance properly. Maybe by their sixtieth wedding anniversary they'd have done this often enough to tear up the dance floor with their prowess.

'Something funny?' she murmured.

'Just thinking of our future.'

'Oh? And how's it looking?'

'Our sixtieth wedding anniversary's going to be a cracker.'

'Slow down. We have so many moments to look

forward to before that.' She slid her hand from his shoulder, down his arm to his wrist, and brought his hand around to her front, placing his palm against her belly. 'You know how we started giving birth control a miss?'

His heart stopped. His feet stopped.

Everything stopped.

Her fingers sliding effortlessly into the spaces between his, caressing her belly, and he tried to speak but he didn't have the words and probably never would have words for this.

'Judah?' she asked uncertainly. 'Breathe. Breathing would be good.'

Breathing could wait. He closed his eyes and used the hand not already cradling their baby to tilt her face towards his. His eyes closed as her lips met his and he didn't care that they were in a public place and that every man, woman and dog could see his tumbling, vulnerable steps towards parenthood. Let them see.

He wasn't backing away from this moment of purest love and worship between him and Bridie for any reason. He was hers.

She broke the kiss, which had deepened considerably. 'Judah, we're in public.'

'Don't care.'

'We're being photographed.'

No flying ducks given. The smile wouldn't leave his face. He was going to be a family man. 'I'd like many children.'

'*So* getting ahead of yourself there on the baby front.'

'How about the kissing front?'

She kissed him again and he lifted her off the ground and whirled her around and she laughed and flung her head back, her hair cascading down her back and over his arms. There was nothing he would do differently when it came to all the decisions that had led him to this moment. Not one single thing.

'I'm so happy,' she said when he finally let her feet touch the ground again. 'You're breathing again.'

He was. Go, him.

'There will be no photos of the actual birth,' she warned, but she fair glowed with happiness. 'I'm beginning to comprehend what it means to be utterly exposed.'

'Not even for the family album?'

She was wavering. He could tell. 'I'll let you know.' She tried for ladylike primness, failed miserably, and he loved her all the more for it.

'Your call, North Star,' he rumbled as they started dancing again. 'But I'm thinking there'll be photos in that album.'

* * * * *

Did you fall into the fantasy of
Return of the Outback Billionaire?
Look out for the next instalment in the
Billionaires of the Outback duet!

In the meantime, dive into these other stories
by Kelly Hunter!

Shock Heir for the Crown Prince
Convenient Bride for the King
Untouched Queen by Royal Command
Pregnant in the King's Palace

Available now!

**WE HOPE YOU ENJOYED
THIS BOOK FROM**

◈HARLEQUIN

PRESENTS

Escape to exotic locations where passion knows no bounds.

Welcome to the glamorous lives of royals and billionaires, where passion knows no bounds. Be swept into a world of luxury, wealth and exotic locations.

8 NEW BOOKS AVAILABLE EVERY MONTH!

#4001 THE SICILIAN'S DEFIANT MAID
Scandalous Sicilian Cinderellas
by Carol Marinelli

When Dante's woken in his hotel room by chambermaid Alicia, he's suspicious. The cynical billionaire's sure she wants something... Only, the raw sensuality he had to walk away from ten years ago is still there between them...and feisty Alicia's still as captivating!

#4002 CLAIMING HIS BABY AT THE ALTAR
by Michelle Smart

After their passionate encounter nine months ago, notorious billionaire Alejandro shut Flora out, believing she'd betrayed him. But discovering she's pregnant, he demands they marry—immediately! And within minutes of exchanging vows, Flora shockingly goes into labor!

#4003 CINDERELLA'S INVITATION TO GREECE
Weddings Worth Billions
by Melanie Milburne

Renowned billionaire Lucas has a secret he *will* hide from the world's media. So when gentle Ruby discovers the truth, he requests her assistance in shielding him from the spotlight—for seven nights on his private Greek island...

#4004 CROWNING HIS LOST PRINCESS
The Lost Princess Scandal
by Caitlin Crews

Having finally located long-lost princess Delaney, Cayetano is tantalizingly close to taking back his country's throne. The toughest part? Convincing the innocent beauty to claim her crown by wearing his convenient ring! Then resisting their very real desire...

HPCNMRA0322

#4005 HIS BRIDE WITH TWO ROYAL SECRETS
Pregnant Princesses
by Marcella Bell

Rita knows guarded desert prince Jag married her for revenge against his father. But their convenient arrangement was no match for their explosive chemistry! Now how can she reveal they're bound for good—by twin secrets?

#4006 BANISHED PRINCE TO DESERT BOSS
by Heidi Rice

Exiled prince Dane's declaration that he'll only attend an important royal ball with her as his date sends by-the-book diplomatic aide Jamilla's pulse skyrocketing. Ignoring protocol for once feels amazing, until their stolen moment of freedom becomes a sizzling scandal...

#4007 ONE NIGHT WITH HER FORGOTTEN HUSBAND
by Annie West

Washed up on a private Italian beach, Ally can only remember her name. The man who saved her is a mystery, although brooding Angelo insists that they were once married! And one incredible night reveals an undeniable attraction...

#4008 HIRED BY THE FORBIDDEN ITALIAN
by Cathy Williams

Being hired as a temporary nanny by superrich single father Niccolo is the only thing keeping Sophie financially afloat. And that means her connection with her sinfully sexy boss can't be anything but professional...

---

*Having finally located long-lost princess Delaney,
Cayetano is tantalizingly close to taking back his
country's throne. The toughest part? Convincing the
innocent beauty to claim her crown by wearing his
convenient ring! Then resisting their very real desire…*

*Read on for a sneak preview of
Caitlin Crews's next story for Harlequin Presents,*
Crowning His Lost Princess.

"I don't understand this…sitting around in pretty rooms and
talking," Delaney seethed at him, her blue eyes shooting sparks
when they met his. "I like to be outside. I like dirt under my feet. I
like a day that ends with me having to scrub soil out from beneath
my fingernails."

She glared at the walls as if they had betrayed her.

Then at him, as if he was doing so even now.

For a moment he almost felt as if he had—but that was ridiculous.

"When you are recognized as the true crown princess of
Ile d'Montagne, the whole island will be your garden," he told her.
Trying to soothe her. He wanted to lift a hand to his own chest and
massage the brand that wasn't there, but *soothing* was for others, not
him. He ignored the too-hot sensation. "You can work in the dirt of
your ancestors to your heart's content."

Delaney shot a look at him, pure blue fire. "Even if I did agree
to do such a crazy thing, you still wouldn't get what you want. It
doesn't matter what blood is in my veins. I am a farm girl, born and
bred. I will never look the part of the princess you imagine. Never."

She sounded almost as final as he had, but Cayetano allowed
himself a smile, because that wasn't a flat refusal. It sounded more
like a *maybe* to him.

He could work with *maybe*.

In point of fact, he couldn't wait.

He rose then. And he made his way toward her, watching the
way her eyes widened. The way her lips parted. There was an

unmistakable flush on her cheeks as he drew near, and he could see her pulse beat at her neck.

Cayetano was the warlord of these mountains and would soon enough be the king of this island. And he had been prepared to ignore the fire in him, the fever. The ways he wanted her that had intruded into his work, his sleep. But here and now, he granted himself permission to want this woman. *His* woman. Because he could see that she wanted him.

With that and her *maybe*, he knew he'd already won.

"Let me worry about how you look," he said as he came to a stop before her, enjoying the way she had to look up to hold his gaze. It made her seem softer. He could see the hectic need all over her, matching his own. "There is something far more interesting for you to concentrate on."

Delaney made a noise of frustration. "The barbaric nature of ancient laws and customs?"

"Or this."

And then Cayetano followed the urge that had been with him since he'd seen her standing in a dirt-filled yard with a battered kerchief on her head and kissed her.

He expected her to be sweet. He expected to enjoy himself.

He expected to want her all the more, to tempt his own feverish need with a little taste of her.

But he was totally unprepared for the punch of it. Of a simple kiss—a kiss to show her there was more here than righting old wrongs and reclaiming lost thrones. A kiss to share a little bit of the fire that had been burning in him since he'd first laid eyes on her.

It was a blaze and it took him over.

It was a dark, drugging heat.

It was a mad blaze of passion.

It was a delirium—and he wanted more.

Don't miss
Crowning His Lost Princess,
available April 2022 wherever
Harlequin Presents books and ebooks are sold.

Harlequin.com